Genesis Encryption

A Sal Luca Gig

By Jon Frazer Langione

PublishAmerica
Baltimore

First printing

PublishAmerica has allowed this work to remain exactly as the author intended, verbatim, without editorial input.

ISBN: 978-1-4489-9094-8 (softcover)
ISBN: 978-1-4489-4599-3 (hardcover)
PUBLISHED BY PUBLISHAMERICA, LLLP
www.publishamerica.com
Baltimore

Printed in the United States of America

To Major David Cohen

Acknowledgment

My loving wife Cathey has worked long hours editing Genesis Encryption. For Cathey's care of my written word, I am deeply indebted. Genesis Encryption could not have been written without her.

The Key

If we have not discovered that which is not in us,
that which is in us, cannot be found.
Marcellus III

Reading that simple quote set me on a journey of discovery. I did not know what direction to take, where to go, or what part of the world I could discover the deeper meaning of that one sentence. I just knew it was profound. Truth be told, I do not have much time for the search. I am a crime reporter for the Philadelphia Daily Editor. But the quote never left my thoughts. No day passed without that riddle coming into my head. It was with me always. The inability to shake it meant one of two things. It mattered or I was ruminating. If I was chewing on it all the time, I would find a way out of it. Realizing this edged me toward the former—it mattered. Then one day, I got a call from a woman who claimed to be an envoy. The envoy told me that my question could be answered. My first reaction was to ask her how she came to know the quote and its impact on me. As a reporter, I learned a long time ago—never ask the obvious questions. Always let the subject speak and never interrupt. So I did. She promised that if I bide by her word she would put me in contact with a 'grand authority'. One who could uncover the secrets? One who would 'peel away the layers'? I had to devote a fortnight to the task. I was overwhelmed. This was it! What I had been waiting for. But I knew it was out of the question to go to my editor to ask for any time off to visit with the grand authority so that I could learn the meaning of this quote that had been with me for so long. I knew he would deny it, thinking me crazy. This had nothing to do with writing a story about crime. But by asking for overdue vacation time since I had only spent three days off in the last five years, I knew he would say 'go ahead' without question. Off I went with his blessing to start this incredible journey, a vacation of a lifetime.

I met the grand authority by being directed to an apartment in downtown Philadelphia. From these words forward, everything is direct quotes from my recordings and my recollections of the encounter. During my 'vacation' I spoke to eight people: The envoy, which remains unidentified, I spoke with only over the phone; the grand authority; a scientist that I met under unusual circumstances; another envoy and the four horsemen. Yes, the four horsemen of the apocalypse.

I was sent a key by courier. It was for an apartment that was on the third floor of non-descriptive building. I was taken aback as I entered. The walls and flooring were bright white with black tiles scattered on the floor, breaking the symmetry. Two white leather arm chairs faced each other with a glass top coffee table between them. I called out to see if anyone was there since no one had greeted me at the door. With no response, I wondered around, checking room to room, in case I had not been heard. No one was in the kitchen, which was as bright white as the first room I entered. It had a kitchen nook. When I looked into the bathroom, it was as white and bright. However, I did notice there were no mirrors which seemed strange. Somewhat puzzled as I went through the place, I wondered into the bedroom. It had a single bed and dresser. Everything in this room was also very bright white. The whole place was beyond hospital clean white. No wall hangings, no greenery, no extras—just the necessities, all in bright white. There was not a window in the place. And like the bathroom, no mirrors. Now, I realized I was closed in from the outside world. But I was not afraid. I felt an unexplainable, comforting essence from the glow of the bright white. On the dresser was a note. It appeared that my many questions about the quote and its meaning would have to wait as I read, 'Have a rest and we will begin at eight on the morrow'. I sat my briefcase down and went to bed.

I was awakened by my cell phone. The envoy told me it was seven and that I was to eat breakfast and be prepared for the interview to begin sharply at eight. I went into the kitchen, where there was a breakfast already prepared for me. I heard no one in the apartment—surreal. Although closed in from the outside world, the door I had entered remained there so I was free to leave. Now, although not seeing anyone or anything, there was a presence in the room. I could feel it.

I sat at the kitchen nook and ate my meal. I looked at a clock on the wall and the sweep second hand was approaching the twelve—eight o'clock. I looked at my watch to confirm the time and out of the corner of my eye, I caught a shadow behind one of the white chairs. I turned to look at the wisp of a shade and before my eyes, a figure developed out of the shadow. Soon, standing before me, was a tall person with a pale white face, robed in a deep crimson velvet cloak. The figure was about six feet tall, had long brown hair with white streaks, eyes gray with gold flecks. I noticed the hands. They were bright white, almost transparent. The face was amazing. Long and lean, with a high forehead and a long angular nose. I could not tell the gender of the figure—a gentle being, moved towards the two white leather chairs I saw when I first entered the place. His figure gestured for me to have a seat. For just a second, I glanced back at the breakfast and the table was clear. I got up and walked over to the chair opposite of the figure. I did not extend my hand. For some reason, I felt it was inappropriate. I sat and the figure sat.

"Good morning Salvatore. I trust you had a good sleep and a filling breakfast."

The voice startled me. It was at once commanding and yet soft and reassuring.

"I did." That was all I could say as a thousand questions spun around in my head.

"Relax. Please, take a moment to gather your thoughts. I want you to lead the discussion. I brought a script for us. You will need this to help you on your quest. So, are you relaxed?"

I realized that it was the figure asking the questions and being very patient with me. I took a deep breath. "May I ask who you are?"

"I am called Helel."

"I'm sorry, but I have to settle down a little. I have never met anyone under these circumstances."

"You have a choice now, Salvatore." Helel said looking toward the door.

I was not about to miss what could be the greatest story of my career. "I have made my decision." I said without moving and Helel could see I had settled in and was sure of my decision.

"And in an answer to your next question which you are trying to frame in a tactful manner, I have no gender. I am an angel and leader of the Nephilim."

I must have had that deer in the headlights look. Helel started to laugh and I started to laugh along. "You got me on that one. The way you appeared, I believe you. I must believe you for all this to work."

"That is correct, Salvatore. You must believe."

"Ah... I am taping this." I pointed to the recorder in my pocket.

"Fine, but you are the only one who will be able to hear what we are about to discuss."

"I can deal with that," I said as my enthusiasm started to build. I was excited to get started.

"Here is the script. I know this is a diversion from your past interviews, but it is important that you stay on track. If we have not discovered that which is not in us, that which is in us, cannot be found, is very profound. It will take a fortnight for us to answer the questions you have for me. That is the reason for the structured interview as outlined in the script. These papers are from a translation. Translating from the original tongue into English is a very precise application. We will not deter from the written word."

"Original tongue? Are we using the bible for this?"

"Discovering that which is not in us is a complicated task. Paraphrasing the text will only confuse the issue and bog us down. I am not trying to lead the discussion. I am giving you the point of reference from which to question me. Have faith. This is the way to the answer."

"So, we are using the bible?"

"The first book of the bible. Bara-shis, it is called. Translated to Genesis."

"You are leading me through the bible, verse by verse."

"In a way you have never imagined."

"To tell you the truth, I have not thought of the bible very much. I am not a very religious man."

"I am not religious at all."

"What?"

"If you want religion, join a church."

"You have no religion?"

"I need none. I am an angel."

"So, what you are saying is that you rise above it all, correct?"

"I am above, if you wish to use that word. I am above it all to the extent that I am eternal. I am immortal."

"How long have you lived?"

"I am from that which is infinite. I have no beginning, nor end. I live in the realm of now. I only use time lines, like the fortnight that I asked you to be here, as a point of reference for you. But, we are getting ahead of ourselves. This is why it will be best to follow the script. Follow the translation."

Helel handed me the papers in his hand. They felt like silk. My initial estimate was that he had handed me over three hundred pages of text. The papers had no weight. As I perused them, I saw that we would be reading a translation and the pages were numbered backwards from an English text. On the right half of the page was the original tongue text and on the left, the English translation. I set the text on the table and picked up the first page. "Should I just follow along?"

"Yes. As we go over the text you will have questions. Many questions."

"Well, let's try a page or two. Kinda get us in sync."

"**The beginning of Iawah's creation of heaven and earth.** This is at the very beginning of the first chapter. It is good to start with verse one, is it not?"

"Yes, a good place to start. I am not all that familiar with the bible, but does it not start with 'In the beginning...created'."

"Good point. See the reason for the script?"

"Yes. But..."

"'Iawah created' is past tense, it indicates a sequence. This version uses the word Iawah, which means of thought and idea. There is no ambiguity. There is no sequence to infinity, timelessness, that which is eternal. This is not a book of history, but a book of humankind's purpose on the Earth with Iawah being the sovereign of the Earth. Keep in mind the idea of humankind's purpose in the universe throughout this discussion. You have discovered a very important tenant for the explanation of your quote. May we refer to it as your quote throughout the interview?"

"My quote. That'll work. So, what you are saying is, there is a sequence to the formation of Earth within the Universe. How can that be?"

"Understanding this is from the perspective of the human reader. You have an understanding of time that is sequential. I understand your understanding, but that is not the way I relate to events. All events are in the now. I am the now. You in your understanding have a past, present and future. It is written from Iawah's point of view and it is important that you grasp that as we go through the development of the Earth, for that matter, all the Universe. Everything is infinite, both forever and now at the same instant."

"I think I am beginning to understand this concept. To me, you realize, it will be a concept, not an absolute?"

"As it should be."

"Go on. If I get lost, I will tell you."

"**...heaven and the Earth—when the Earth was void....** This is an explanation of a void. The something of nothing."

"Whoa. The something of nothing?"

"A state of wonder. The wonder of the void. You see, nothing is something. Like your quote. Without something, you cannot have nothing. Stick with me here. In order to have that which is, you have to have that which is not. In order to have something, you must have nothing and in order to have nothing..."

"You must have something."

"Right. So, you see, the nothing was something in the context of nothing needing something and something needing nothing to exist."

"They can't exist, one without the other?"

"Good, very good. And that brings us to the next little matter. That which is good."

"How so?"

"We will get to that shortly. Let me continue....**with nighttime on the surface of the deep, and Iawah hovered over the surface of the waters...a**re you following? Nighttime was present because there was no light."

"I grasp that, but where do the waters come from. Wait a minute. There was no solid earth so that which is not solid, has to be, in order to have solid. But, we have not gotten to the solid yet."

"We are going to be there very quickly. You are doing quite well, if I do say so."

"So, the surface of the deep is dark space?"

"Correct. We've got two things to look at already, four actually. Dark, no light; surface of the waters, no waters. In the absence of..."

"Gotcha."

"**Iawah said, "Let there be daytime, and daytime began.**"

"Just for my own reference, we now have void and water as the surface of the deep, and light and dark. I'm with ya."

"**Iawah saw that all was good, and Iawah separated between the nighttime and the daytime.** Now, we are to the point of the word good and its meaning in the context of the creation story. Iawah saw that all was good comes up several times. Good in this context means...let me ask you, have you ever done something and when you were finished with it, you held it up and said 'good'?"

"Yeah, sure."

"That is the context of good."

"A statement of completion?"

"Right. In this case, the item under discussion, is complete. It is not the opposite of bad. Iawah makes nothing bad. Iawah does, however, complete....**called to the light: "daytime," and to the dark Iawah called, "nighttime." And there was nighttime and there was daytime, 'a full day'**."

"Hum. I'm going to have to think this through a bit. Sounds like we have a time line here?"

"Yes we do. The time line is for humankind. It is a reference for that which has yet to be created. This creation, thus far, could have been in the wink of an eye or in a millennium. Those are your time references. Genesis was written for you. Theories abound that the universe was a coincidence or chaos. Genesis refutes those theories. I do believe we should take a break for now. Take a breather."

"In my time. Not in yours since there are no hours in your time."

"Very good, Salvatore."

"Please, call me Sal."

"Done."

"And all was good."

"I thought it would be good to take a break after the creation of 'a full day'. To let you digest quite a bit of information. I must say, you picked up on the concepts very well. And now, since you have a rudder on the ship so to say, we can talk about thought, idea and concept. For that is what the first creation story is about. All of what we shall discuss in this, the first story is a thought and an idea of Iawah. That thought develops into an idea and then a concept is formed. But the conceptual creation story comes later."

"You mean the first creation story is not real? Only a thought and an idea?"

"When you put words on a paper, type them out on your computer, are they real?"

"Yes."

"After the words are on the paper are they more real than the thoughts behind the words' creation?"

"I think I can understand where you are going with this. Please, continue."

"What you may feel is real is the word on the paper. But you do not believe that anything before that one word is real. The word was merely a thought. You give more importance to your explanation of real then to the thought, do you not?"

"Yeah. I guess I do."

"I tell you this, the thought is just as important as the word on the paper. They are both real, one as the other. It is a human trait to believe that real is only what can be touched, or at least seen."

"How is that?"

"Why is it that all dramatic situations are considered reality? I often hear the anguished cry out that their situation is real. Are we not real just being here today?"

"Okay, let me see if I got this straight. Real is, is. If something is, it is real. The mere thought or idea or concept of a thing makes it real?"

"You are getting a handle on it. What I am getting at is the thoughts, ideas and concepts of Iawah are as real as the light and the darkness, the surface of the waters, all real."

"What I am understanding is that the light, darkness and waters are only in thought, not yet put on paper, so to say."

"Precisely, Sal."

"You know, I go through each day trying to find things, crimes mostly, to write about. I have been at it for so long I just go through the motions. I do it without thinking. I am on autopilot. Now, I have been enlightened more than I have in years I am enjoying this."

"Oh, but there is more. Let us take on 'another day' shall we?"

"I am all for it. Do you want me to follow along on the script?"

"Please. **Iawah spoke, "Let there be an arc of the sky among of the waters, and let it divide water and water.**""

"Okay. What is the arc of the sky?"

"The arc of the sky is the atmosphere that surrounds the world, the Earth. **So Iawah made the arc of the sky, and divided the waters which were beneath the arc and the waters which were in the sky. And it was."**

"It was. I take 'it was' has the same connotation as good? In other words, it is done?"

"You are correct."

"In thought and idea?"

"That too, is correct. **Iawah called to the arc of the sky: Heaven**."

"So, all of the air, all of the atmosphere is heaven. But it sounds to me that the waters are the Earth, the orb. The arc of the sky is the air. But I am confused about the above and below. I can see above the waters, but below what?"

"The clouds, the moisture in the air, are also water are they not?"

"So, atmosphere is a better term then air?"

"As a point of reference for our discussion, yes."

"And it seems to me that the atmosphere between the clouds and the water orb is what Iawah called heaven."

"Ah. But you missed this one. Iawah called the arc of the sky heaven. Iawah calls that which is heaven a much different place then you, I mean, the way humankind refers to heaven."

"Okay, let me see if I get this. There seems to be a fine line on this one. It seems to me that the heaven we are speaking of is the atmosphere above the surface of the waters, right?"

"That is right. So, we have only defined the heaven to which Iawah spoke. Let us not get ahead of ourselves on this heaven thing. Above the waters and below the clouds is our reference for another day. **And there was nighttime and there was daytime, 'another day'.**"

As Helel was quoting verse, I was looking down at my script. When I looked up Helel was gone. I read my notes and added to them the lessons of the day and the many questions I had to ask Helel the following morning. By the time I had this accomplished, it was ten at night and I fell into bed with a head full of new thoughts, ideas and concepts. "What would tomorrow bring?" was my last note.

Then There Were Three

When I went out to the kitchen Helel was sitting there. I had written down many questions and wanted to get through them before the script work began. Helel nodded that it would be appropriate. I sat across from Helel and we began.

"You said you were the leader of the Nephilim Were they not fallen angels? Men who had relationships with women? Therefore, you are male, are you not?"

"I can come from the spirit in any form I wish. My charges chose to incarnate and come to Earth to know women. I, however, did not. But, Sal, my friend, you are getting way ahead in the interview. I tell you this; your eyes will be opened to all these wonders when we speak of Noah. I am androgynous. I have been, always."

"Thank you. I take it we will continue with the script?"

"True. **Iawah spoke "Let the waters under the heaven accumulate into an area, and let the dryness appear.""**

"Ah, we have another reference to heaven. In this context heaven means the atmosphere below the clouds, does it not? Is it cloudy all the time? Are the clouds a constant? The clouds are water vapor and nothing is there to dissipate them?"

"That's right. There is no sun. The sun hasn't been created yet, has it?"

"That begs another question. How can there be daytime with no sun, that is, if the sun has yet to be produced?"

"With each question, you are confirming my choice of you for this message. I am very pleased. But, to the daytime. The nighttime was the void, the nothing, yet without the void we cannot have that which is not a void. The void is referred to as nighttime; the daytime is the illumination…the daytime…the light of understanding…"

"…of thought and idea. Excuse me for interrupting. But the first day was no thought and thought. With no thought there could then be thought?"

"Very good."

"Ahah. But now the problem is presented: a problem in my mind not in the quotation. Without that which is not we cannot have that which is. A paraphrase of the Marcellus III quote. So the air is, the atmosphere is, because that which is not air, water, is. Yet, now we have dryness appear, a whole new addition to the, is, is not, reference."

"You do not have to have two to tango, as you say. In this case, you have three to tango. The dry land is not water nor is it air. Air is not dry land nor is it water and water…well, you see my point. This is known as a triad, a group of three. Even though there is a threesome, it still fits within the confines of your quote."

"I guess I was getting a little two dimensional about my reference to the quote. Sorry."

"No need to apologize. That does bring up another good reference. That of height, width, and depth. Another triad. **Iawah called dryness, "Earth," and to the gathering of waters Iawah called, "Oceans."**"

"I noticed that on the script you have Iawah and Iawah is spelled with an I not a Y. And you never refer to Iawah as 'he', why is that?"

"There is no translation of Y in the original tongue. Therefore not Yahwah, but Iawah. The correct interpretation is the letter I. And also, Iawah has no gender. I know that using he is a common reference in other versions of Genesis."

"Are you saying whoever wrote this, Moses if you will, wrote it incorrectly?"

"No, I am saying that there have been edits to the bible. Again, I restate, Iawah has no gender."

"I take it, or at least I feel a point will be made about this as we progress?"

"Sal, you are getting it. You are staying in the moment with the lessons. And they are lessons, are they not?"

"Indeed."

"And Iawah recognized that it was good."

"Done."

"You will discover that the next day is a very busy day. A lot will be revealed. **Iawah spoke, "Let the Earth grow vegetation: herbage having seed, and fruit trees having fruit after its species, having its seed." And it was. And the Earth sprang vegetation...**"

"Whoa. How can we have vegetation without the sun?"

"Have you ever watched a plant mature and overnight it sprouts anew and you can tell the amount of growth it attained in that one night?"

"I see your point. As I reread this verse, I also see the after its species. What is the meaning of this?"

"Iawah has decreed boundaries for the atmosphere, waters and dry land. Iawah has also defined boundaries for the vegetation. Each plant will be pollinated by its own. It is to keep the fruit pure, to keep it from getting tainted by cross pollination, if you will."

"Sort of like the term kosher?"

"In the original tongue, yes. In English, kosher means proper. So, in that context it would be correct to say, after its species, keeps it proper. I never thought of it that way until now. Good point, Sal."

"Please, go on. Sorry to interrupt."

"**...herbs having seed by its species, and trees bearing fruit, each containing the seed of its species. And Iawah saw that it was. And there was nighttime and there was daytime, 'another day'.** A very busy day indeed. Iawah made way for the development of land, vegetation, and for the survival of animals and ultimately humans. So, now, do you want to take a break?"

"Not at all. Please, let's continue."

"You are finally getting your sun. **Iawah spoke, "Let there be lights in the arc of the sky of the heaven to divide between the daytime and the nighttime; and they will be signs, for days and years; and they shall be as lights in the arc of the sky to shine upon the waters and the dryness." And it was.** I can see you straining at the bit."

"I love how heaven is developing. I take it heaven, or better stated, the heavens are expanding, but days and years."

"Later in the development of humankind came the calendar and even the wristwatch you wear today. Keep in mind that time, as you know it, is a human realm only. So, what are these lights?"

"I would say the reference is to the stars which would shine or rather be seen only at night and could be used to divide the day from night. As Iawah says, they shall be as lights, they, being plural. If I am correct, the sun and the moon were created separately."

"You are close. Iawah has yet to create them. But, as you will see, Iawah did not make them. They, the stars and the moon and the sun were already created. And that shall be next. **Iawah allowed the two lights, the light of the daytime and the light for the nighttime and the stars to shine through.**"

"I see. This is a very good example of the thought and the idea. Iawah making the first daytime and nighttime was the thought and the idea. What about the concept?"

"That comes in the second creation. The putting of the word on the paper, so to say. **Iawah set them in the arc of the sky of the heaven to give daytime on the Earth, and to give nighttime, and to divide between the light and the dark. Gehova saw that it was. And there was nighttime and daytime, 'another day'.**"

"So the whole thought of light and dark, night and day came upon Iawah on the very first day of creation?"

"The thought of the entire creation came upon Iawah in an instant or a millennium. The story of creation is broken into a time line for humans to understand the development. The luminaries were created in thought 'one day', but were set in place on 'another day'. All was created, and then set in place when it was so determined. Thought to idea. Now, Sal, I am sure your notebook will be filled tonight and you will have many questions for me tomorrow. Take a break. Go out tonight. Have dinner out. See you in the morning."

And with that I watched Helel fade away and be gone. I went to dinner.

Think Hard Quickly

After I finished breakfast, I sat to review my notes. It was past eight and I wondered where Helel was. As soon as I framed the order of my questions and reviewed the script, Helel appeared.

"Why are there no windows in the rooms?"

"If light shows through, I cannot be seen. Do you see any light fixtures on the walls or hanging from the ceiling?"

"No, but as I was ready to go to sleep the light dimmed. At seven in the morning the light appeared. It was automatic to my schedule, just as the breakfast."

"There are no light fixtures, as I am the light of the rooms. If sunlight came through windows, I cannot be seen."

"Why is that?"

"Have you ever seen an angel before?"

"No, I don't think I have."

"We are all around. You cannot see us, as we do not present ourselves incarnate."

"Why did you choose to make this interview session only two weeks long?"

"This will be a life changing event for you. This exposure to your question, your Marcellus III quote, will be unfolded and you will walk in a different light. Even now, what we have discussed has had an effect upon you and from that you cannot go back. It is kind of like the Mafia, you so often write about."

"Genesis and the Mafia. That is a strange combination."

"I do not mean to combine them. I am merely saying that your involvement with me is like the Mafia. Once in, you cannot get out.

You know too much. Sal, you know too much. I dare say, you know more than any theology scholar will ever aspire. How many do you know with the experience of an encounter with an angel?"

"No one that I know of. Not in a same context, outside of the bible that is. I don't know if I would believe them if I heard or read about it or someone told me."

"Sort of like the people that have alien encounters. It is a matter of creditability."

"Yes, I guess so."

"Well, let me enlighten you. Very few on this Earth will believe you. There are always those who choose to believe in anything. There conviction is surface and readily seen as a ruse. They fool themselves. You will be badgered by them as much as those that will not only doubt you, but will condemn you."

"Are you telling me this experience is mine and mine alone?"

"Yes. The publication of this interview is up to you. I am just telling you the truth as to how it will be received. Those on the fringe and those that will condemn you are out there. And the mainstream will not understand. You have got to put this interview, these two weeks, into lay terms. Do not try to cross into theology, as all theology has an agenda."

"An agenda?"

"Yes. An agenda of proof. The deepest believers are also the greatest skeptics. Theology is not the study of the divine, it is the study of the science of Iawah. You can only learn from the creator who created all."

"The bible is interpreted in so many ways. I do get your point about the agenda. Should I publish this...well...some will say I have an agenda."

"To sell the story."

"True and to unlock the Marcellus III quote. An agenda that is both business and personal."

"All humans have an agenda. No human is without an agenda."

"Do you have an agenda?"

"No. But I do have a mission. I guess the best word is mission. And that mission is to enlighten you, not the world, you."

"All of this is for me and me alone?"

"Kind of makes you feel special, does it not."

"No, overwhelmed."

"You need not feel that way. I chose you to receive the lesson. If others wish to believe you, or mock you, it is theirs to do. And you will."

"I will what?"

"Speak the truth."

"Whew."

"Shall we continue my friend?"

"By all means."

"Iawah spoke, "Let the water swim with creatures, and birds that fly over the Earth, within the arc of the sky in the heavens.""

"Heavens, not heaven?"

"Keep in mind that what we covered yesterday expanded the light and the darkness. The arc of the sky went beyond the closeness of the space between the clouds and the waters or dry land. Heaven in the atmosphere and heaven above the atmosphere, that is, the universe and beyond, the infinite. Heaven below and heaven above. Thus the heavens. Heavens."

"Got it."

"Iawah created huge fish and ocean mammals and creatures that creep, with which the water swam after species by species; and birds of every kind. Iawah saw that it was. Iawah blessed them and spoke, "Multiply, and fill the oceans and the arc of the sky.""

"'Fill the 'oceans'? Iawah called the gathering of the waters oceans. Were the oceans, unlike the heavens, created all at once?"

"Exactly. I think I am getting an idea of why you are wrestling with the idea of heaven so much. Do you believe that heaven is a place?"

"I do. Is not heaven where you go if you are good, if you pass muster, so to say?"

"No."

"Just no, can you expand on that a bit?"

"Just exchange the word heavens for skies."

"Are you telling me that what we believe to be heaven...the great reward is not a place. In what context does it exist?"

"Heaven, as you are thinking of it, exists in no place. You cannot go to heaven any more than you cannot go to hell, if that is the connotation in which you are thinking."

"I print this I'll be stoned."

"Probably."

"There was nighttime and there was daytime, 'another day'."

"I think I just noticed something."

"The days?"

"How'd you guess?"

"I am divine."

"Now you are cracking wise."

"No, I am stating the truth."

"It's the ending of the 'days'. It is almost as if there is no commitment. Iawah ends with 'a full day' or 'another day'. Meaning in each case, 'on each day', it was not 'the day'. It was 'another day'. Just 'a day'. Oh well, I guess I'll create the world in 'a day' or so...just 'another day'."

"Now who is cracking wise?"

"Not really, but it does beg the question. Were those days just 'another day'? Were there other days before them or after them?"

"You are really getting on track now. You are thinking on all cylinders."

"How so?"

"I was wondering when you were going to get around to it."

"The idea of other creations."

"Yes, but you have been very good at staying with the script. This takes us a little off script. But go ahead."

"I was always under the impression that the world, Earth was created in concert with the rest of all creation. I guess I felt the world, our world, was the focus of all of creation. That it was all created at once."

"There is a sequence to the creation, but this applies only to the creation of Earth. Remember, we talked about that in the very beginning of the interview."

"I recall that, but it did not dawn on me until we embarked on 'the days' thing. What you are telling me is that this is the story of the creation of my world, the world in which we live? The Earth and the heavens that surround it. That is a tiny bit of the universe, is it not?"

"How does that make you feel?"

"You sound like a shrink."

"Sorry. I could not help but ask that. How does that make you feel, really?"

"Small, sort of. I mean, I thought that we were all a part of the big plan?"

"You are. You are walking in the light every moment of the day. You just do not realize it. At the end of this, you will. To answer your basic question. The world was created for you. That should make you feel very important, special, unique...you are, you know?"

"Thank you."

"You are welcome."

"Which brings me to ask you another question?"

"Go ahead. Ask away."

The scripts you have given me are in small increments so I cannot read ahead. I am assuming you have purposely done this so I will stay focused on the topic you have planned for us to talk about, so I won't miss the finer points along the way. As you can tell, with each bit of information you have given me, I want more. My problem? There is so much to digest in such a short time we have together. I was wondering if our sessions could be longer. I even wish that I did not have to stop to sleep or eat."

"That can be arranged, if you would like."

"Having the sessions extended would give me more time to answer my questions.

"I can do you one better. I have the ability to grant your wish of not eating or sleeping."

"That is great, but what is the catch? Will I crash after twelve days of no food or sleep?"

"Still concerned with "if it is too good to be true, there is something wrong?" No. I would not do that to you. No, I am going to bring you into my realm of time. No day, no night, no time, no need to eat and no need to sleep. And to top it off, you will still have your twelve vacation days."

"Saying wow to an angel does not seem quite right, but I'll say it anyway. Wow and thank you."

"You are welcome. Are you ready to continue?"

"Can't remember a time that I was not ready to have an opportunity to do this story. Please, let us continue where we left off."

"Iawah spoke, "The Earth is to bring about living things, according to its species, animals, and crawling things, and beasts according to their species." It was. Iawah made the beasts on Earth, species by species and the animals of their species,..."

"Let me pause a moment to think this over. Is there a difference between beast and animal?"

"Yes. The beasts are wild and the animals are tame, to be domesticated."

"Ah, got it."

"**...and beings of the ground of their species. And it was.** Just as the fish, birds and vegetation, the beasts, animals and things that crawl on the Earth stay to their own species. I anticipated your question."

"Do you know every question before I ask it?"

"No. What free will would you have if that were so? You have surprised me with your depth of understanding. Our interview is going well."

"I'll say."

"If you have enjoyed yourself up to this point, you are going to love the up and coming. **Iawah spoke, "Let us make man in our image, to our likeness. They..."**"

"Whoa! 'Let us... in our image... to our likeness'. Us and our. That's a plural. We are in Genesis and there is now more than one Iawah. How is that?"

"I would have bet my wings that the verse I just read would bring you out of the chair. It is paraphrased: 'And Iawah said to the ministering angels who had been created on 'the second day' of creation of the world, **'Let us make humankind.'**"

"Where in 'the second day' of the creation are angels mentioned?"

"Remember our discussion about the days, 'another day', and so on?"

"Yes."

"See in the script. It says 'another day' not 'the second day'."

"What you are telling me is that there is more than one creation sequence? I know the question sounds systematic."

"You are correct. Angels were created on 'the second day'. I know, I was there."

"Yeah. I guess you were."

"Iawah told Moses when Iawah came to create humankind, Iawah took counsel with the angels."

"I'm with you and was that man, Adam?"

"You are getting way ahead. Look at the script. It says make man. Not make a man."

"Subtle, but point made."

"It is in the context of humankind."

"I'm back on the script."

"Good, let us continue. **They will have power over the fish, the birds, and over the animals, all of Earth, and things that crawl on the ground.**"

"What about beasts? They are not mentioned."

"What wild animals did man, back then, rule. It took millennia for man to conquer the wildest of beasts. Yet, today, does man rule over the tiger or the polar bear and others of cunning and power."

"Only with a gun, I guess."

"More is the pity for that, too."

"**Iawah created man in Iawah's likeness, in the image of Iawah created man, male and female.**"

"I know before I ask, I'm gonna be off on the wrong track. But I have to ask. Do we look like Iawah? Does Iawah look like us?"

"Not in features, but in morality, reason, and free will. I do not know of any physical likeness of Iawah. I have never seen Iawah."

"If you have not seen Iawah, how can we?"

"No one can see Iawah. One can know Iawah. To know is better, is it not?"

"And Iawah created male and female. What about the whole rib thing."

"Really, Sal. You keep getting ahead. The script."

"Okay, back to the script. I thought I knew a lot about the bible. Like most people do, but I feel like a newby."

"Don't be so hard on yourself. More will be revealed."

"I am ready for it to be revealed."

"**Iawah blessed them and Iawah spoke, "Multiply, fill the Earth and subdue it; and have power over the fish, the birds, and every living thing that moves on the ground.""**"

"That would include the beasts, would it not?"

"Enough with the beasts, already."

"Okay, okay."

"You crack me up. **Iawah spoke, "I have given to you its species bearing seed, and every tree that has seed in its fruit; it is yours for food. To every beast, to every bird, and to everything that moves on the ground, all have a living soul, and you have vegetation to eat." It was.**"

"It sounds to me as if humans were to be vegetarians. And also, that animals, for that matter. And all living things have a soul?"

"Vegetarians indeed, you are correct. Why would not animals have a soul?"

"According to many religions, only humans have a soul."

"That's nice. **Iawah saw what was made, and it was done.**"'

"This time, it was done."

"Iawah is speaking of the entire creation, not just 'that day'. **There was nighttime and daytime, on 'a sixth day'.**"

"On 'a sixth day', why so defined? If I am correct, and I am cautious to say this. The days defined as 'another day' could have time spans in between, but on 'a sixth day' defined a specific day when all was done.

"You have the gist of the time line."

"The gist is that there was no time line for six different days."

"You got it."

Rest Ye Merry

"The day of rest is brought about by Iawah having completed Iawah's work on 'a sixth day'. **Thus heaven and Earth were complete, and all that was done. On 'a seventh day' Iawah had completed Iawah's work. Iawah made 'a seventh day' a day of rest and blessing.**"

"This is the reason for the Sabbath, rest, is it not?"

"True."

"But many religions rest on Sunday, the first day of the week."

"That's nice."

Made Manifest

"These are the creations of heaven and Earth when they were created on the days The Gehova made heaven and earth..."

"The creations being what was made manifest on those seven days?"

"Correct."

"The Gehova as opposed to Iaway? Why The Gehova?"

"Iawah is expressed in the first creation story of thought and idea."

"Ah. We are getting into the second story?"

"Yes...follow on your script. You may wish to go back a bit to see the difference. Remember, we talked of thought, idea and concept."

"I'm at the first day of creation."

"A good place, hold onto that thought. The mind first thinks. Then the mind conjures an idea. Iawah is the thought..."

"...and idea."

"Right. Iawah of the first creation story. Iawah of the mind. The Gehova is the manifestation of the creation."

"The concept. Thought, idea, concept."

"Very good, Sal."

"But how can that be? I thought according to the scriptures there is only one? But now, as I understand, there is Iawah of thought and idea and another, in this case, The Gehova, of the concept. Is there a difference?"

"Iawah and The Gehova are one."

"I am trying not to get confused."

"Try to follow. You are Sal. When you are forming a newspaper story in your mind are you not Sal, the thinker? Then, you put the words to paper and are you not Sal the writer? And then you become Sal, the editor. Albeit, a simple comparison, you get my point."

"I see where you are coming from."

"It is the same in that Iawah is the thinker. Iawah then has the idea. Then, The Gehova is the manifestation, the same as Iawah. The Gehova, of the concept made into substance. Iawah the thinker forms the idea, The Gehova brings the concept into being."

"Why was not the first chapter of the script called, Iawah's Creation, or something like that? Now, with the substance being created, the first creation story being brought to, I want to say reality, but that is not quite the word. Two creation stories..."

"Okay, I see where you are going. It was the writer that labeled the chapter. Genesis, meaning origin or source. What you are thinking about is what was The Gehova before Iawah of the creation, since we seem to have several states of the same being."

"I hope I am not confusing you by going back to the beginning. What was Iawah before Iawah the thinker, Iawah of the thought of the creation? You, the angels were created on 'the second day' were you not? Iawah was then The Gehova of the angels' creation."

"Yes, you can put it like that. And I have no knowledge of The Gehova before that, before the concept of bringing me into being. Just as you are the thinker, writer and editor. The realm is of the angels, the substance of the world in which you live, and the manifestation of all that is. Time and no time. Things and no things."

"I think I am getting a handle on this. But some religions separate them into say father, son and holy ghost."

"Iawah is the same as The Gehova, whether Iawah is being The Gehova of a father figure, The Gehova in the son form or The Gehova of the spirit. In this case, it is a matter of interpretation. There is only one Iawah or The Gehova."

"Whew. I get it."

"That was not too hard, was it?"

"You had me going for a bit. I am having fun with grasping all this. You put it all into such simple terms."

"Not really. The thoughts, ideas and concepts are all very easy to understand. It is the mind of humankind, the concepts of humankind, that is in variance with the truth. I speak only the truth to you. That you understand so well is a tribute to what humans call open minded. You are very open minded."

"Thank you."

"You are welcome."

"So The Gehova has now made Earth and heaven in substance."

"All will be manifest in substance. Let me continue. Follow on the script if you like. **The trees in the fields were not on the Earth and the vegetation had not yet grown, for The Gehova did not send the man, for the man was not there to farm."**

"So, the concept, the development into substance, is following the thought and idea into substance, in the order of the first creation story."

"Much along those lines, yes. Man has not been manifested. That is to come in two verses. **It rained and watered the soil. The Gehova formed the man from dust of the Earth, and The Gehova breathed into the man's nostrils the man's soul, and the man was alive."**

"I see here that only man was made manifest. In the first creation story the thought and idea gave us both male and female."

"I understand what you are getting at. You know I formed the script in such a manner that you may not read ahead. I did this for a purpose. Some of the substance of creation is a bit out of order to the thought and idea. No animals have been made manifest. In due time. In human time. From here on out, until the tenth chapter of Genesis, we will be discussing and unfolding the development of humankind. Until humankind is responsible for its own spirituality."

"Responsible for its own spirituality?"
"More will be revealed."
"Will you stop saying that."

A Little Light Gardening

"I see by the script we are going into the garden."

"Shall we? **The Gehova planted a garden in Eden, to the east, and placed there the man.**"

"So, The Gehova made the man outside the garden."

"The Gehova did so, that man may experience that which was not the garden in Eden. Garden 'in' Eden. Not, garden 'of' Eden. I thought you might bring that up."

"To the east of what?"

"East means that which is within the kingdom of The Gehova and west means that which is without the kingdom of The Gehova. Let us continue and we will have our bearings. **The Gehova caused to grow every tree that was a pleasure to see, and for food, the Tree of Life grew in the center of the garden, and so was the Tree of the Knowledge of Good and Bad.**"

"I thought it was the tree of good and evil."

"Evil is a state in and of itself. Good is the opposite of bad. Good without bad and..."

"...you cannot have good. Without the one you cannot appreciate the other. I am finally getting a handle on this."

"I must say, you are."

"And of the tree of life in the center of the garden?"

"It represents the center of life. The tree which all the branches of man's being will grow. Now, onto our geography lesson. Shall we?"

"Can't wait."

"**A river flows from Eden for the garden, and from there is separated and becomes four branches. The first is Pishon.** Let me stop here and explain. Every word...every word of the original tongue from here on out has a translation, a meaning. So, I will stop periodically and translate for you. The meanings are very important to your understanding. You shall see."

"You are talking about Pishon."

"Correct. Pishon is (being). Let us move on. **Surrounding the garden is the river Havilah,** meaning (trouble), **where there was to be found gold.** Wait. Stay with me a bit. **And bedolach,** (bedellium), **was there, and shoham stone,** (onyx). Now, your question."

"Gold. There is a reference to gold and I take it precious gems? What would be the value?"

"The connotation is that life is precious. Keep with the meanings. So far, we have 'trouble' and 'precious'."

"Can you give me a sec to change to a fresh tape? We seem to be entering a new realm, as you say?"

"Of course."

"Good to go."

"**Another river was Gihon,** (formative movement), **it surrounded a land called Cush,** (darkness). **Another river was Hiddekel,** (rapid spiritual influx)...**it flowed east of Assyria,** (the soul), **and the last river is the Euphrates,** (the blood stream).

"Having the meanings of these words casts light on the whole story. I thought that they were place names. Names on the map."

"They are names on the map. Do not confuse the names with the locations. Theologians, the scientists, do that. Yes, there is a river named the Euphrates. And a country named Syria. The names of those places were taken from the scriptures. Not put into the word by any proximity."

"So, where was the garden in Eden? Where is Eden?"

"Eden is the place where your quote of Marcellus III came to be. 'If we have not discovered that which is not in us, that which is in us, cannot be found." We have come to the point of the formation of humankind, in body and in mind."

"In body and in mind. What about spirit?

"We have a long way to go to get to the point of humans being responsible for their own spirituality."

"I know, you mentioned that before. I have faith that more will be revealed."

"Very good, Sal. Very Good."

"Is there, or was there, an actual location of the garden in Eden? An actual location of Eden and all these rivers?

"If there was a physical location, would it not have been wiped out by the flood? We are getting ahead of ourselves by about four chapters. I think, though, that there is a need to discuss this geography question. Many biblical names are used to name places. Let me put it this way. There is a Goshen in both Indiana and New York. Is the land of Goshen in either?"

"No. I think not."

"That is just an example of the myths of locations of biblical place names. In Israel there are seven different mountains named Sinai. Which, if any, is real? You get my point. No location in the original tongue can be exactly attributed to any geographical location on Earth. Not even Egypt. Trying to interpret those locations takes from the meanings as we have started to explore."

"Theological scientists, again?"

"Correct. Stay with me, Sal, and follow the meanings. Are you ready to continue?"

"Of all we have talked about, I think this will bring the most heat. The most trouble from the theological community."

"Yes. You are overturning the life's work of many scholars and they will not be pleased. Truth disturbs many. Truth is the light and many have been wondering in the land of Cush."

"Darkness."

"Indeed. To get us to a sound basis, I think I will interpret the meanings a bit more. The context of the meaning is important to continue."

"I think that may help as I feel I am only getting the surface, not the whole context. Context is a good word. I need the context of the Garden in Eden."

"So, here goes. Cush is darkness, but not just dark. Cush is the lack of enlightenment, whereas Eden is the place of enlightenment. Without the lack of enlightenment you cannot have enlightenment. The first river mentioned is Gishon or formative movement, the development of humankind and the environment. Then, follows the river Hiddekel, which means rapid spiritual influx flowing east into Assyria; presenting spirit to, not instilling spirit in, humankind. This is the beginning of the development of the spirit of humankind and of all living things."

"But I thought you said that humankind is not yet responsible for its spirituality."

"Humankind is given a soul and spirit, but it will be a long time before the spirit becomes the triad of humankind's body, mind and spirit. Body and mind first. Fourth we have the river Eupharates, the blood stream. The flowing of life through the body."

"So, as I see this, the mind is yet to be developed."

"The first human has a mind, a brain with which to think and realize the surrounding. But, and this is a big but, the mind is not developed, as you say. You will see. Remember our likeness discussion we had, in the likeness of morality, reason and free will? These have yet to be given to humankind. Let us continue. **The Gehova placed the man in the Garden of Eden, to farm it and to protect it."**

"Now, we have the Garden 'of' Eden, as I see in the script. The garden of?"

"The Gehova has placed the first human in the garden of enlightenment. From outside of the garden, the land of Cush, or darkness, to the land or garden of enlightenment. Do not get too caught up in this. Yes, we have the light, no-light. This is not, however, the darkness and light you are thinking of. I can see you are wondering as to the depth of this. Right, now it is only dark, not knowing, and light, knowing. We are not yet into the deeper meanings of reasoning, morality and free will. We are getting there. **The Gehova spoke to the man "You may freely eat of all the fruits of the trees; but of the Tree of the Knowledge of Good and Bad, you will not eat; when you eat it you shall die."**

"I understand that The Gehova instructed. The Gehova left no alternative. It seems to me that this would have been enough to keep the first human from eating from the tree."

"It did, for awhile that is. And you notice again we have good and bad, not good and evil. Evil is a state of being that has no opposite save for The Gehova. Evil is an illness. A state of the unhealthy. There is no have, and have not, for it."

"Good, I get it. Now, it says you will die. I interpret that to mean death will be brought upon you as a state of being, not that the first human will die immediately upon eating the fruit."

"Precisely. So, as this is instructed by The Gehova and the first human understands the ramifications, I can tell you this. That in the absence of life there would be no death, in the absence of death there would be no life. The first human lived to be nine hundred thirty."

"So, what you are saying is The Gehova knew that the first human was going to violate the instruction."

"The whole garden, the whole of enlightenment versus the whole of Cush, the whole of darkness, was created to give the first human an understanding. The Gehova understood, as did we."

"Angels, then, knew how this was to play out?"

"Yes."

"Had angels been through this? Were you given instructions to break, to understand good from bad?"

"No. We were blessed with the understanding without having to take a fall, so to say. The fall had to happen. It is the reason for it that may shake your former understanding."

"Trust me. A lot of my former understandings have been shaken. It is as if I was to understand things incorrectly to understand them correctly."

"You could put it that way. **The Gehova spoke, "It is not good for the man to be alone, I will make a mate for the man.""**

"Two things here. One, is it bad that man is alone, instead of 'not good'?"

"Not in this context. You could say it was not pleasant. But I am going by the exact interpretation. And what is your second point, let me guess."

"Go ahead, guess."

"Man versus first human."

"There is only the man and not yet a woman?"

"Yes. Whence comes the woman I shall refer to them as man and woman. We are getting there. Follow on your script. **The Gehova had formed out of the Earth every living thing, and brought them to the man so the man could name them, and whatever the man called them it was their name. The man gave names to all living things, but as for the man, the man had no mate."**

"I'm a bit confused. In the first creation story, male and female were made according to the thought and idea. Yet, now the concept has these difficulties."

"In the first creation story, the male and the female were developed, but not in the depth and breadth we shall soon see. There was no Cush or Eden. There was no good or bad. We are developing humankind to the fullest potential. True, Iawah created them in Iawah's image of morality, reason and free will, but only in thought and idea. This is the concept and the giving of humankind morality. Reason and free will is being accomplished in a manner of steps. That is a good term. Step-by-step."

"More will be revealed."

"Exactly.

This Shall Be Called

"The Gehova caused the man to sleep; and halved the man. The Gehova formed the half into a woman, and brought her to the man."

"'Took half...there is nothing here about a rib. I was taught that woman, Eve, was fashioned from the man's rib."

"That's in error. In this case, it's a demeaning idea that woman would be formed from only a small part of the first human. Woman is equal in all things to man. Woman was created from a half of the first human. The first human was called man. Never is it written that the first human was a man. Man was referred to as 'the man'. No name had yet been given and the man was not described as naked until after woman had been created."

"Are you implying that the first human, the man, may have been androgynous? No gender existed until the cleaving of the sleeping human?"

"Did not Iawah say, 'Let us make Man in our image, in our likenesses on 'the sixth day'? Did not Iawah take counsel with the ministering angels?"

"What you are saying is that the first human, the man, was created in the form of an angel. Was an angel sent down unto earth and placed into the garden? If that was the case, would not the man be all knowing and have all the mysteries already unlocked?"

"No, the first human, the man, was not angelic. Only in the physical does the man have incarnate features of the angel form. I do look somewhat human, do I not, sitting before you in this form?"

"Yes, as I see you now. But you flow in and out from the invisible to the flesh."

"And that is what the first human did. When The Gehova cast a deep sleep upon the man, he slept. The first human was not torn apart physically…no need for that. The first human was made to fall into a deep trance and from there was formed both man and woman. In the form I am before you and then placed in the garden. I am spirit incarnate. I am a spirit made more dense. I am not flesh. I am spirit in a form to be recognized by you. I am before you, no one else. If there were others in the room, they would not see me. The man was before The Gehova. And, of course, The Gehova saw the man. When The Gehova took a side of the man, The Gehova filled it with flesh and so at that time the man was no longer ethereal, but man was brought about in flesh. The man was not man in the flesh until the creation of woman. It is the culmination of the genders created incarnate"

"The concept was fulfilled."

"**The man spoke, she is of our bone and of our flesh.**"

"I think I've got it. On 'the sixth day', where it says male and female, Iawah created them. They were created in thought and idea, not even in the spirit of the angels. This creation story has the first human coming from thought and idea to an ethereal concept to being created in the flesh with woman. Both of the same proportion and therefore, being equal. You know this equality thing is not going to fly very well. There is a huge difference between this interpretation and the other versions of the book of Genesis. I'll probably get stoned again for this."

"Metaphorically speaking."

"Let's hope so.

"**She was called woman, and from the man she was taken. And man will leave his father and mother, cling to his wife and they shall become one.**"

"Yes."

"This, keep in mind, was the original development of gender. As in 'the man' to a man and a woman. Henceforth, the man will be no longer referred to as the man but man and woman."

"That's means they are fully in the flesh."

"You are correct. I did it as much to keep my place in the story as I did to differentiate for you. **They were both naked and not ashamed.** Keep this verse in mind, as we will come back to the ashamed, again. Being ashamed later is an indicator from The Gehova that will play a huge role in a future discovery. Okay, to the next chapter in your script please."

Cunning Is as Cunning Does

"**The Gehova made the serpent to be the most cunning of beasts.** We get back to your beasts, again."

"What I was talking about earlier was man controlling the beasts, or lack of control. But, now, with the word cunning what comes to my mind is that the serpent, the beast, will control humans. In this case, the woman. So, the serpent was the most cunning creature made by The Gehova?"

"By far the most cunning and because of the serpent, you get a giant leap closer to having your quote unfold before you. Love the serpent."

"Love the serpent? Okay, I'll take your word for it."

"Good. **The serpent spoke to the woman, "Was it not that The Gehova spoke: 'Eat of no tree in the garden'?"** The give away in this verse is the 'no tree'..."

"Perhaps The Gehova did or didn't. The woman should have picked up on that right away. And the serpent leads her to believe the serpent understands that from every tree fruit can be eaten."

"Pulls her right in."

"I could write a story for the Daily Editor about this. The biggest con of all."

"Keep that idea in mind. You may wish to do that. On a slow news day, that is."

"**The woman replied...**"

"Sorry. Let me interrupt here. The first person to speak, other than The Gehova is the serpent. I just realized that. In the absence of that which is, we have that which is not. I think I know who the

serpent is. The serpent is what The Gehova is not. Of course, The Gehova is all things, but in this context that which is not The Gehova is evil. With our discussion of good and bad and your definition of evil, well, I understand why you made that point. Good-bad, The Gehova-evil. Am I on the right track?"

"Looks like you really want to get into this serpent thing."

"Yeah. I'm likin' this. Now you really got me stirred up."

"Let me get back to where I was...**The woman said to the serpent, "From all trees we may eat. But the fruit of the tree in the center of the garden, The Gehova spoke, do not eat nor touch it, you will die.""**

"How does the woman know of this? Was it the instruction given the first human by The Gehova that was transferred to the woman when man and woman were made from 'the man'. Am I on track here?"

"Yes, perfectly. In effect, that instruction, that admonition, was the first communication The Gehova had with a human. It was also the only communication until the serpent spoke to the woman."

"Is there a reason the tree is in the center of the garden? Other than to give its location for the restriction?"

"The tree is the center of that which is the life force of man and The Gehova. The branches spread to the domain of The Gehova and it was planted on Earth at the center of the domain of humankind."

"And to just touch the fruit. That is really heavy."

"Indeed. **The serpent spoke to the woman, "You will not die; The Gehova knows that when you eat it all will be revealed and you will be like The Gehova, knowing what is good and what is bad.""**

"This is a set up. The woman is with a man with which she has yet to communicate. She is awed by The Gehova and now she is told she can be like The Gehova; have the knowledge of The Gehova. And really, the serpent is wrong as to the die part, but, is right on the mark as to the knowing of good and bad. The first

communication with man is by The Gehova, the first communication with woman is with the serpent that is evil. Could not this very well have been the other way around?"

"As you shall see, it will be. Follow me on the script. **The woman saw the tree was good for eating and that the tree was a means of wisdom, and she touched and ate the fruit.**"

"She really didn't have to eat it, when she touched it, her eyes were opened."

"**She gave it to her husband and he ate. Their eyes were opened and it was then they saw their nakedness; and they sewed fig leaves and made aprons.**"

"Is this where you meant by the other way around? I think that the man had the choice to say no."

"Yes, and no. Yes, he could have said no and the woman would have gone away from him as he knew not of the ways of their world. But, he had a bond to the woman and wanted to have his eyes opened, also. She did not die before him, so he thought the warning was not creditable. He did not yet fear The Gehova. Until he touched and ate the fruit, then he was in fear. Neither had known fear. All they knew was the perfection of the garden, the love of the creation of themselves in the garden and the relationship to the magnificence of The Gehova. They had not known of that which is without The Gehova. That was the serpent. The serpent gave them fear. The Gehova is magnificence, the serpent is evil and fear. The fact that they were naked is only a metaphor for now knowing evil and fear. They were ashamed of what they had done. Until that time they knew no shame. They also did not know that which was not shame."

"So, their eyes were opened to that which was good as well as bad?"

"The tree of the knowledge of good and bad. This is the most incorrectly interpreted part of the creation story. They knew not bad, but they also knew not good. How can you know good without knowing bad?"

"From what I have learned so far, you can't."

Responsibility

"They heard The Gehova in the garden as nighttime fell; Here is a good point to keep in mind. The deception by the serpent was done in daylight. Not skulking around in the dark of night that we usually think of evil. The night is not evil as the day is not evil. **They hid from The Gehova behind the trees in the garden. The Gehova called to the man, "Where are you?"**"

"The Gehova couldn't find him in the garden? Surely The Gehova knew where the man and woman were. And why does The Gehova call out only to the man?"

"This is another metaphor. When The Gehova asked man where he was, The Gehova meant what state of mind was he in. The Gehova spoke to man, as to him was given the instruction not to eat of the tree. It was man who told woman of the instruction. The Gehova first held man responsible. **Man replied. "I heard your sound in the garden, and I was afraid and naked, so I hid from you."** Man has now realized what he has done. But he knew what he was doing when he did it. He knew he was naked. He was revealed. Man knew he was revealed as soon as he ate the fruit, touched the fruit, and his eyes were opened. **The Gehova spoke, "Who told you, you were naked?"** The Gehova knows that man's eyes have been opened as to the knowledge of good and bad. He wanted man to admit the error, the breaking of the instruction. **Did you eat from the tree, the tree's fruit I instructed you not to eat?** The Gehova knew the answer. This was a test of the taking of responsibility of man for his actions. **Man replied, "The woman who is with me—she gave me the fruit, and I ate it." The Gehova spoke to the woman, "What**

have you done!" Note the exclamation mark. The Gehova is showing emotion as to the gravity of this event, but more so by the two of them laying the responsibility off on each another. **The woman replied, "The serpent deceived me, and I touched the fruit. And I ate the fruit.**"

"They sound like they both need to go to co-dependents anonymous. He's punkin' off the woman and she is droppin' a dime on the serpent."

"Now, ask yourself this. How can these two be responsible for their own spirituality?"

"I see your point."

"The Gehova spoke to the serpent, "Because you have done this, cursed beyond all beasts, upon your belly shall you crawl, and you will eat dust all of your life.""

"Something tells me that the serpent has not yet died."

"How did you come up with that?"

"Because we are still cursed with evil in the world."

"Sal, you are the man. **I will put ill will between woman and you, and between your offspring and men's offspring and women's offspring. They will beat you, and you will bite them.**"

"Offspring?"

"Hang in there. We will get to the offspring. **The Gehova spoke to woman, "I will increase your pain in childbearing. Yet you will desire your husband, and he will rule."** I can see you straining at the bit again. He will rule, means that man will be physically stronger. This is another one of those misinterpreted verses. This verse has caused a lot of consternation for woman in the world. There is a chauvinistic interpretation of this that misses the mark by a mile. In many countries throughout the world this is used to oppress woman and that is evil."

"Whoa. Helel, don't hold back. Say what you mean."

"The Gehova spoke to Adam,"

"Adam, where did that come from, out of the blue?

"Adam means both human being and Earth. Adam was not a full human being until The Gehova named him so. Adam now has the body and mind of a human knowing good and bad. By his body, he will till the Earth, by his mind he will know the good and bad throughout his days. ..."**because you allowed your wife to have you touch the fruit of the tree of the knowledge of good and bad, cursed is the ground because of this. You shall toil all your days. Thorns and thistles will sprout, and will choke out the vegetation that grows. Through this toil will you eat only bread and return to dust, the dust from where you came. You are dust, and to dust you will return.**"

"Kind of makes farming a weary task."

"It is."

"And dust to dust?"

"Only The Gehova comes from the unspoken. We, the angels are all derived from that which is spirit. Here's a question for you. What is material?"

"That which is not spiritual."

"Good. So, when man was first created out of the dust, man became incarnate. That which is material. Does it matter that man was made of dust and we, angels are made of another substance, say ether, in the form you see me now. Man was made of dust to return to dust."

"So, what you are saying is that The Gehova knew man would cause man's own mortality; that man would fall in the garden. The Gehova knew this would happen all along. Is that what you are saying?"

"Of course, The Gehova knew the way events would proceed. The Gehova knew, but the woman and the man did not know."

"Did the serpent know which way the woman and the man would react? Did the serpent know that up front?"

"The Gehova and the serpent knew from before the beginning of time that woman and man would fall, as you say. It could not turn out any other way. Did you notice that The Gehova became emotional. The Gehova knew that the two of them would not own up to it."

"If this was preordained, so to say, why all the creation and the development of the life forces used to support the humans? Why not just do it?"

"But it was just done. The story of it is for your understanding, your learning. Have you not gotten a lot out of our interview so far?"

"Yes, I have. And I could not have grasped any of this without the step by step through which I have been taken. Thank you."

"You are welcome. **The man called his wife Eve. She became the mother of all that was living. The Gehova made skins for Adam and Eve and clothed them.** From now on, when I come to a name in the script, I will give you the meaning. The meaning has a very deep bearing on the text. So, we see Adam is a human being and Eve is elemental life. Two very good starting points. **The Gehova spoke, "man has become unique, knowing good and bad;"** the unique is the serpent and The Gehova. The Gehova and evil, the superlative of good and bad. "**So man and woman would not live forever by taking from the tree of life!"** The second time The Gehova shows emotion. If woman and man would have eaten from the Tree of Life first, they would have lived forever, but would have not known of the good and the bad. Would not have known the very purpose they were put here for."

"No kidding. I need to have more of this revealed."

"And it shall. **The Gehova took him from the Garden of Eden to toil as a farmer. And having driven him out, The Gehova stationed east in the Garden of Eden a Cherubim and the flame of the ever-turning sword, to guard the Tree of Life.**"

"It reads that only he was banished from the garden, did not The Gehova banish the woman?"

"Woman was the correspondent of man and she accompanied Adam. Adam was the one banished because it was he that broke the instruction. The instruction that was given him directly from The

Gehova. And east of the Garden of Eden was the good side, east being good and west being bad in the connotation of direction."

"Who was a Cherubim? I know they are some of the angels in paintings, but who are they specifically?"

"The Cherubim, or rather the meaning of Cherubim is one that intercedes. Along with the Seraphim, the Cherubim are of the first hierarchy of angels. Before you ask, I am a Seraphim.

"You mean I got a top guy?"

"You deserve nothing else."

Oh, Brother

"Adam knew Eve and she bore Cain, saying, "I have acquired a man. Man was from The Gehova."

"She knows The Gehova?"

"Humankind has yet to invoke the name of Iawah or The Gehova. The Gehova represents the infinite one. Eve recognizes that it was The Gehova who gave her the man in her life. Not that there was anyone else to choose from. The thought and idea of the creation is lost in the concept. Eve knows only of the concept that brought her about. She knows The Gehova. She knows not Iawah of the thought and idea. She only knows of the creator of the concept."

"You told me to follow closely the names as they give depth to the creation story. Cain means?"

"Very good."

"Wait a sec...let me get this straight. Eve does not know Iawah?"

"Don't get too far ahead. But humankind will know Iawah as The Gehova until after the flood. We are making a huge leap here. Can we get back to Cain?"

"Sorry. Okay, Cain."

"Cain means possession. The deeper meaning is selfishness. We will see that Cain brought trouble upon himself because of his selfishness. Let us continue. **She bore his brother Abel. Abel became a shepard, and Cain became a farmer and tilled the ground.** Abel means breath or life energy."

"An odd combination, selfishness and life energy. If man does not yet know spirit, or has yet to be filled with the spirit, then the

life energy is the energy that allows life not spirit. Does Cain represent physicality?"

"That is a good way to put it. Cain, as well as Abel, Adam and Eve do not yet know Iawah, only The Gehova. As you will see with the next verse. **After some time, Cain brought an offering to The Gehova, an offering of grain and Abel brought the choicest newborn of his flock.** Do you see the difference with the offerings? Cain brought grain, but not the best grain. But with Abel, the choicest of the flock was offered. The Gehova sees this. **The Gehova turned to Abel and his offering, but to Cain's offering The Gehova did not turn.**"

"Okay, bear with me on this. The Gehova turned to Abel and his offering. Was The Gehova incarnate? How did The Gehova turn to anyone, if not in the body?"

"Abel, as well as Cain, knew of the presence of The Gehova. Turning to the offering is in a metaphysical sense. Metaphysical is an overdone word. Supersensitive may be a better choice."

"So, Cain and Abel were aware of a presence?"

"Correct."

"And Cain was aware he was being spurned?"

"Correct. **Cain was annoyed and became rude.**"

"Rude?"

"Look it up in the dictionary."

"I don't have a dictionary."

"Look to the right side of the chair, on the floor."

"Go figure. Of course."

"Well?"

"Course, vulgar?"

"The Gehova spoke to Cain, "Why are you so vulgar? If you improve, you will be forgiven. But if you do not improve, sin will befall you. You can conquer it although it possesses you.""

"Sounds like mental health counseling. So, The Gehova is telling Cain that, if for his next offering, Cain brings the best of

the best, Cain will improve. That sin will not follow him. Is this the first time the word sin is used? I think it is."

"Yes, this is the first time sin is mentioned. This is a good time to talk about the notion of original sin. The Gehova never told Adam or Eve that their actions could bring about a sin. I know you have heard sin means, to miss the mark. And that is correct within this context. When The Gehova told Adam not to eat of the tree of the knowledge of good and bad, the warning was that Adam would surely die. The Gehova never said, that to do so would be missing the mark. It was death that Adam and Eve brought upon themselves. They did not sin. They died the moment they touched the fruit. They brought death upon themselves, not a sin as was pointed out to Cain. Big difference. A sin is forgiven, not death. Cain had the ability to conquer his vulgarity. Not so with Adam and Eve. They did not become vulgar and possessive. The Gehova did not call the acts of Adam and Eve sin. The Gehova did give a warning to Cain about sin. Cain had only to improve himself. The Gehova tells him he can conquer it. But, by the virtue of his name, he is possessed, selfish. Not only selfish with material things, but selfish in his being. He is emotionally headstrong and selfish with what he wants. In fact, Cain cannot face the truth of his own lack. He lives for the now, lives for immediate gratification, as opposed to in the now which is emotionally healthy. Cain is so emotionally torn that he becomes a criminal. One characteristic of a criminal is that they live for immediate gratification. They live for the now."

"I know Cain killed Abel. But why? Was it not to Cain who The Gehova spoke and told him to improve himself? Why did he take it out on Abel?"

"Good questions all and we shall discuss them in a moment. **Cain spoke to Abel. Abel was in the fields of the flock, Cain raged against his brother and killed him.** Cain killed Abel because Cain felt that it was his brother who caused The Gehova to condemn him for not bringing the choicest offering. Cain blamed Abel for his problems in that if Abel would not have brought the best of the livestock, Cain would not have been made to look bad. In Cain's eyes, he looked bad because of Abel. In effect, Cain did not take responsibility for his actions. Cain lived in his own world of blaming that which is outside himself."

"It's strange that Cain does not blame The Gehova, also."

"Oh, but he does, he does. **The Gehova spoke with Cain, "Where is your brother?" And Cain replied, I do not know. Am I my brother's keeper?"** This is not the first lie."

"What then is?"

"The first lie was when Eve blamed the serpent, as if the serpent made her do something. Eve said she was deceived, yet she was told not to even touch the fruit. And then, we have ol' Adam, he puts it off on Eve. The only one to be in the good graces of The Gehova is Abel and for that, he was killed. Persecution would you not say?"

"Sounds like it to me."

"**The Gehova spoke, "What have you done? The voice of your brother's blood cries out!"** On your script, you see The Gehova expresses emotion. To Cain, The Gehova says. **"Therefore, you are cursed more than the ground you till which has soaked Abel's blood. When you till, the ground will no longer yield grain. You will become a vagrant and roam the Earth.""**

"Sounds like Cain is being condemned to be a street person. Is that the only punishment for a murderer?"

"That was all that could be done considering that there are no police, courts or prisons. Cain thinks that is too much. Let us look at this from the stand point of The Gehova. The Gehova wants to punish Cain, but in so doing, The Gehova wants nothing to befall Cain. Follow along. **Cain said to The Gehova, "My failure is too much to bear."** Cain thinks the punishment is too much for him, another trait of the criminal. Somebody is always pickin' on me. **"You have banished me—can I be hidden from you?"** Well, this is another overstated cry from Cain. He was not banished from the Earth. He was punished to wander it. And now, Cain worries about his own death. Again, another criminal trait—self-centeredness. You can write the book on criminal behavior with Cain and the way he sees things. **"Am I to become without a home and roam the Earth?"** See, he admits he is not banished from the Earth. He answered his own question. **"But I could be killed!"** Again, already with the drama. Everything with this guy is taken to the extreme. But, The Gehova recognizes that Cain has a point."

"Wait a minute. But I will be killed? Who can he run into but his mother and father?"

"Wait, it gets better than that. **The Gehova spoke to Cain, "Whoever kills Cain, through seven generations the killer will be punished." The Gehova put a mark on Cain, so that Cain will be recognized and not be killed.**"

"Where do these people come from?"

"More will be revealed."

"There you go, again."

"Cain left the presence of The Gehova and lived in Nod, east of Eden."

"Okay, let's back up a bit. The mark of Cain, I thought was to be a punishment. You hear that a lot. He or she has the mark of Cain. But actually, this was a protection given Cain by The Gehova."

"Correct. A much misinterpreted quote."

"Then it is written that **Cain left the presence of The Gehova**. *What does that mean?"*

"It means that Cain's wandering had started. As you see next, Cain settled in Nod. And before you ask, Nod means wandering with uncertainty. So, Cain settled into wandering in Nod, which is also a land of good."

"Eden was in the east and was good, so the land east of Eden must, also, be good. The Gehova condemned Cain to live on the good side."

"Bravo. Cain's punishment was reform, rehabilitation, getting his act together."

"I am still trying to figure out who the slayers could be."

"Get a load of this. **Cain knew his wife, and she bore Enoch.**"

"Ah, come on! Where did the wife come from?"

"No one knows. It has never been written and neither Iawah nor The Gehova explain that phenomena in the script. Many guesses have been made, but none hold water. It is a great mystery. I am sorry, but this goes unanswered. And, Enoch means founder. It denotes a new state of thought. Cain becomes a city-builder. **Cain was a city builder, and named the city Enoch, after his son.** You will find that many cities are named after persons of the times. Sometimes it tends to get a little confusing, but I will keep you on track. We will get into the begots every now and then. I will tell you the meaning of their names as we go along."

"Fair enough."

"And when we do this, I shall point out how the meanings, as to the name, and as to the city, differ."

"Differ?"

"Yes, in the case of Enoch, (founder) and the city Enoch, (centralizer)."

"That makes sense. Bringing people to the city, the center of commerce. This thing about where these people came from really bugs me."

"You'll get over it. And in this case more will not be revealed."

Then Began the Begots

"Understanding the meanings of the names and cities will open your eyes as to the development of the traits of humankind. Each name is a condition of humankind. We have gone from Cain, body, to Abel, mind, to Enoch, founder, and now**...To Enoch...Irad.** Irad means self-leading passion which gives in to foolishness, stubbornness and confused thoughts **Irad begot Mehujael** meaning the belief that power and strength are physical**...Mehujael begot Methushael** meaning man of The Gehova."

But keep in mind that man is yet only mind and body**...Methushael begot Lamech.** Lamech means strength and health...Lamech was anything but healthy as you shall see. **Lamech took wives: One was Adah** meaning beauty as in the beauty of love; **the second was Zillah.** Zillah is gloom; the gloom of living in the physical, having no spiritual nature. See, we get back to that, and will, time and again."

"It's as if humankind is being reminded of the lack of spirituality with each generation."

"You will see that a generation is almost a millennium. So, it takes quite awhile to go from generation to generation, and when seven generations are cursed, it takes a long, long time to get out from under the spell."

"Seven generations?"

"Remember, 'whoever slays Cain before seven generations have passed he will be punished'?"

"Ah."

"**And to Adah, Jabal;** Jabal meaning abundance, **the first to**

raise cattle. His brother was Jubal; meaning melody, **Jubal was a musician, he played the flute and harp.** Jubal represents harmony by the expression of musical instruments. **To Zillah was born Tubal-Cain** meaning diffusion of Cain which represents a greater selfishness, a broadening out, **he sharpened tools of copper and iron.**"

Tubal-Cain's sister was Naamah. Naamah means social unity. **And Lamech spoke to his wives, Adah and Zillah, hear me: I have killed a man by my wound and killed a child by my bruise? Cain suffered vengeance at seven generations, and I Lamech will suffer seventy-seven!** Tubal-Cain lead his father Lamech as Lamech was blind. Tubal-Cain saw what he thought was an animal and asked his father to shoot the animal with an arrow. Lamech did. In so doing, killed Cain. Lamech was so distraught that he flailed the air. In so doing, killed Tubal-Cain. Lamech's wives left him. His punishment was many times seven because he killed his sons by accident."

"It seems that it is a greater sin to kill by accident than to take a life on purpose."

"It would seem as though."

"But would not Tubal-Cain be responsible for the killing of Cain?. He told his blind father to shoot the arrow?"

"But it was Lamech, the blind man, who decided to shoot at what he could not see. Thus, making a bad choice and being very irresponsible. No, it was Lamech that killed Cain. He could not lay it off on Tubal-Cain. Just as Eve could not lay it off on the serpent and the same thing as Adam with Eve. You will see as we move on in the script that this responsibility thing comes up time and again. The difference is that humankind was not yet responsible for spirituality. Spiritual matters were not within their authority. Humankind was given responsibility for acts of the mind and body, and that is where we are right now, the beginning of the begots."

"I have heard this referred to as the begats."

"That's nice."

"What do you mean 'that's nice'?"

"It is the wrong word. Begat means archaic while begot means to procreate as the father. You tell me."

"I see your point."

"**Eve became pregnant, and she bore Seth.** Seth means compensation. Let us continue...**The Gehova has provided me another child in place of Abel, who Cain had killed.** You can see from this, although Abel and Cain are now dead, Adam's affection still goes to Abel."

"Could it not be that Adam is leaning toward the cerebral? The mind, rather than the body? Thought over power?"

"Good analogy. **Seth, begot a son and named him Enosh.** This is a big one, Enosh means a mortal, miserable man. It is what happens when a man sees all he has built up is nothing compared to the spiritual link with The Gehova. At his wit's end, does man call on The Gehova. It is that man has tried everything on his own, and has come up short, failed, leaves nothing but the worldly and now calls out to The Gehova instead of walking through his life without The Gehova at his side. The Gehova is always at our side. It is we who care not to walk with him. And humankind suffered for that and it explains the next verse. **To call out to The Gehova was profan**e."

Lineage

"I see by the script that we are now getting into the begots big time."

"And now we may be able to shine some light upon the dilemma of your struggle with the wife of Cain. Just when she was created. **Here is the account of the descendants of Adam—on the day that the man was created by The Gehova, The Gehova created the man in the likeness of The Gehova.** Follow real close. This is real subtle. **Created were them, male and female.** Is the plural them for the two of them, male and female or is it for both male and female, as in The Gehova created them male or The Gehova created them female. The plural of both male and female. Males and females. This is the only indication that more than one of each gender was created. This is the only explanation of the creation of the wife of Cain. **They were blessed and called man,** meaning humankind**, when Adam was a hundred thirty years, he begot Seth,** Adam's compensation."

"Could not the wife of Cain been a sister? A girl born to Eve?"

"This is a theory put forth by many theologians trying to pin this matter down. But nowhere is it stated that Adam and Eve parented a girl before Cain died. I think it is unwise to add what fits in the mind of the theologian just to prove a point. Nowhere in the book of Genesis does it give credence to that theory. Adam and Eve did have sons and daughters. Follow along. **Adam lived for eight hundred years after he begot Seth and he begot sons and daughters.** See, it was after Cain was killed. **Adam lived nine hundred thirty years; and died.**"

"After nine hundred thirty years? Are these years in our years, according to our calendar?"

"Yes, there comes a time when lives are limited to one hundred twenty years. We will get to that. **Seth lived one hundred five years and begot Enosh.** We are now getting into the lineage of the survivors."

"Survivors?"

"Abel had no progeny. Cain's lineage perished in the flood. Only Seth's survives. The genealogy begins with Seth through Noah and his sons. Again, a lot more of this later. Oh, and remember Seth's son, Enosh, is a miserable, mortal man."

"Are not all mortal?"

"No..."

"More will be revealed."

"Real good. Continuing...**Seth lived eight hundred seven years after he begot Enosh, and begot sons and daughters. Seth lived nine hundred twelve years and died.**"

"**Enosh lived ninety years and begot Kenan,** meaning being a self-centered one. Do you see how this trait of Cain's continually flows through his generations? You will see it again. **And Enosh lived eight hundred fifteen years after he begot Kenan, and begot sons and daughters. Enosh lived nine hundred five years and died.**

Kenan lived seventy years and begot Mahalalel, the might rising or glorification of the Gehova. **Kenan lived eight hundred forty years after he begot Mahalalel, and begot sons and daughters. Kenan lived nine hundred ten years and died.**

"Mahalalel, sounds like the word hallelujah comes from that name. To praise The Gehova."

"It does. **Mahalalel lived sixty-five years, and begot Jared,** descending, meaning The Gehova descending, or the acknowledgement of The Gehova by man. **Mahalalel lived eight hundred thirty years after he begot Jared, and begot sons and daughters. Mahalalel lived eight hundred ninety-five years and died.**

Jared lived one hundred sixty-two years and begot Enoch, meaning in this case, repentant.

"Is it through the Jared's Enoch that the sins of Cain are forgiven?"

"That is one postulation. As you will see what happens to Enoch. **Jared lived eight hundred years after he begot Enoch and begot sons and daughters. Jared lived nine hundred sixty-two years and died.**

Enoch lived sixty-five years, and begot Methuselah, man of the sword, meaning the swiftness of the pierce of the sword as in the power of life. **Enoch walked with The Gehova for three hundred years after he begot Methuselah and begot sons and daughters. Enoch lived for three hundred sixty-five years. Enoch walked with The Gehova. Enoch did not die, he was taken by The Gehova.**"

"So, Enoch did not die but was taken. So, where did Enoch go?"

"Into the spirit to be with The Gehova."

"What about the others that died. Did they not go into the spirit of The Gehova?"

"The difference is they had to go through the pain of death. Enoch did not."

"Was not Enoch just as dead as the others?"

"No, Enoch was in the spirit as were the others. But Enoch did not go through the pain of dying."

"So, all dying is painful?"

"Extremely so. It is the gnashing of all sin within the body. Then comes the release into the spirit."

"How long does this pain last?"

"A blink of an eye or a millennium. There is no time in the spirit world. If you are worried about suffering, do not. The Gehova does not cause the dead to suffer."

"How then do we atone for our sins?"

"You atone for your sins by your consciousness on the Earth. There is no punishment in the spirit."

"So, you are saying we are not condemned to everlasting suffering for our transgressions?"

"You mean sent to the infernal regions, forever?"

"Yes."

"Good grief, what would be the point? And there is no such thing."

"What you are saying is that heaven and hell do not exist in the context of what many have been led to believe?"

"We already discussed the meaning of heaven, air and the skies. And hell is in your head. 'There is no heaven or hell but what we think it'."

"Shakespeare."

"About sums it up."

"But if we don't have a system of punishment or damnation, how do we bring humankind into the fold of The Gehova?"

"How are you doing so far?"

"I see your point."

"Let us move on and get to Noah. **Methuselah lived one hundred eighty-seven years, and begot Lamech.**"

"Another Lamech, strength and health?"

"Good, you remembered. **And Methuselah lived seven hundred eighty-two years after he begot Lamech, and begot sons and daughters. All the days of Methuselah were nine hundred sixty-nine years and he died.** Methuselah, the power of the sword to the glorification of The Gehova, was the longest living human.

Lamech lived one hundred eighty-two years, and begot a son who he called Noah, saying, "Noah will bring us rest from our toils and our curses and he called out to The Gehova.""

"Lamech invoked the name of The Gehova. Was he not punished for it?"

"No. Lamech was speaking of the future of Noah as the great

shepherd of humankind. It is through Noah that man becomes all that we are today. **Lamech lived five hundred ninety-five years after he begot Noah and begot sons and daughters. Lamech lived for seven hundred seventy-seven years and died.**

At five hundred years of age Noah begot Shem, Ham, and Japheth."

"I take it you did not go into the meaning of Noah for some reason."

"Noah means rest, calm and peace. You will see that Shem will represent the renowned. Ham will represent the warmth of life, our living body, and Japheth will represent intellect."

"You said will represent. They do not yet represent what their names mean?"

"No, they will represent the ultimate triad. But let's discuss the story of the flood. Keep in mind the meaning of the names dealt with the physical. Humankind is in the selfish fight for life. Like an organism using all its energy to stay alive no matter what, man is of the same nature."

From Creation to Population

"Witness what the people suffered by not having a spirit. **Daughters were born of man.** Man refers to humankind and daughters refers to the general population. **The sons of rulers...**the rulers were the princes and judges."

"Where did they come from?"

"A lot can transpire during the five hundred years of Noah, you know, when he had his sons. A lot of begots happened during that time. And they set up societies. When you do that, there are those that rise in the community to lead."

"I'm with ya."

"And the sons of rulers...**saw that the daughters of man were good and they took them as wives.** The use of good here implies that the relationship would be good and not in the sense of good and bad; from the tree. **The Gehova spoke, "I will not contend with this!**"

"Ah, now I get it."

"The not contend is that The Gehova will not allow this to go on. And that humankind is in the flesh. Having no spirit, no link to the eternal good, humankind cannot not fail. It is inevitable, the progression toward the spirit."

"It is almost as if it were preordained?"

"Not really, but it was expected. Humankind has the free will given by The Gehova at the creation. Humankind has chosen the route, to which you will soon see, ends the flesh. The flesh will be destroyed to be made whole. I see you are shaking your head."

"More will be revealed."

"the days of man and woman will be a hundred twenty years."

"Yeah, that must have raised havoc with social security. One hundred twenty years is still quite a life span."

"It meant that The Gehova would wait one hundred twenty years before the flood was brought upon the people. The Gehova gave the people one hundred twenty years in which to repent."

"Did the people know that this was the time frame to repent? It is not written in the script?"

"They had free will, remember, and it was up to them to become that which was good by the tree. The people knew of good and bad as the eyes of Adam and Eve were opened to it."

"And yet they still failed. I guess you could call it failed. They failed to be drawn into the fold of what was good. But did this not become more difficult by the meaning of the names in the begots? I seems the people were destined to fail as the flesh, the sins of being in the flesh, compounded, generation after generation."

"But think who compounded it with the lineage. The names were given the progeny by the parents. The parents compounded the effects of the flesh. But keep in mind, they had no spirit."

"If they had no spirit, how could they be held responsible for that which was spiritual? The defining of good and bad is in the spirit, is it not?"

"The knowledge of the tree of good and bad is in the mind, flesh and spirit. The spirit, however, is the closest to the good of The Gehova, the magnificence of the creator. The people have to go through this rendering to get to the spirit."

"It seems they, the people, were created lacking."

"Back to the tree. Adam and Eve had the choice."

"The light just went on. The creation of humankind was not complete when Adam and Eve touched the fruit. They preempted the process. Am I on track here?"

"Essentially. The knowledge of good and bad would have been given them as the creation process went along, but they preempted the process. Preempt is a good description. Now to my guys."

"Huh?"

"**The Nephilim lived on the earth...,** The Nephilim represent the spiritual ideas of The Gehova as the sons of The Gehova."

"What does Nephilim mean?"

"Fallen angels. **The Nephilim consorted with the women. They were mighty angels of war and devastation.**"

"Please, can we take this one step at a time?"

"The Nephilim were on the earth in those days, as it was me who sent them. They were shepherds of the flock, spiritual shepherds, if you will. In accounts of their coming to Earth, it was said the people were but grasshoppers next to them. They were giants."

"Why was it that they did not fulfill the task to provide spiritual guidance to the people? Were they to provide it to all of humankind?"

"I'll answer your second question first. Yes, the Nephilim were sent here to shepherd all of humankind to the spirit. Humankind had no internal spirit as you do today. Humankind was bad to the point of wickedness and the Nephilim could not reach into them, into their very being to give them the guidance that was needed. So bad, so wicked, was humankind, that their wickedness fell on the fallen angels and the Nephilim in turn became tainted. They mated with the women and taught humankind the skills of war. Both heinous acts. The Nephilim were mighty, but their spiritual being could not overcome the people, so wicked were they. **The Gehova saw that there was great evil on the Earth.**"

"This is the first time evil has been mentioned among humankind. Had they gone from bad to evil?"

"Yes, they were indeed evil. Criminal to the last, save one, and we will get to that one. **The Gehova considered what The Gehova had done and had remorse for the creation of man.**"

"What you are telling me is that The Gehova was disappointed with the creation of humankind. How could The Gehova have made, have created, something or someone not to The Gehova's liking? Couldn't The Gehova just change it?"

"There would be no point of the true magnificence of The Gehova if The Gehova made man in The Gehova's likeness without free will. The Gehova has free will and so does humankind. It was humankind that sought after the knowledge of good and bad. It was humankind that found out that good and bad exist in man. It was humankind that preempted The Gehova in the development of the appreciation of good and bad. It was humankind that spoiled the discovery. And now it is humankind, the people, who must face their wickedness."

"So, allow me to digress. It is the women who are blamed for consorting with the Nephilim? Is it all of humankind getting the blame for learning the skills of war?"

"Yes."

"How can that be so? The Nephilim were just as much a part of it."

"The Nephilim were there to shepherd the people into the spirit. The people chose to behave in a wicked fashion."

"But did not the Nephilim have free will?"

"No. Angels are all within the spirit of the magnificence of The Gehova. We have no free will."

"You had free will to do this interview."

"Who told you that?"

"You mean you were sent here to do this interview?"

"Just as I sent my Nephilim to shepherd humankind."

"Huh? That sure does put a whole new light on things. It is as if we are special, having free will. Are we, along with The Gehova, the only ones with free will?"

"Yes."

"But why? What is so special about us?"

"Nothing. You cannot know the magnificence of the glory of The Gehova if you do not know that which is not magnificent."

"Humankind has got to know that which is not The Gehova, to know The Gehova?"

"You cannot know that which is, if you do not know that which is not."

"As Marcellus the third said, 'If we have not discovered that which is not in us, that which is in us, cannot be found'."

"We are now embarking on the deepest meaning of that very quote. **The Gehova spoke, "I will destroy man who I created and all living things of the Earth and in the sky."**

"Brought on by the preempting of the knowledge of good and bad. Humankind has no depth, are of mind and body only."

"Sal, you are really getting into this."

"I'm in such good company."

The Good Noah

"**But Noah found grace with The Gehova.** The Gehova of the concept, of mercy."

"Mercy! The Gehova is about to condemn humankind to death."

"Yes, but I waited until now to point that out as I knew you would come up out of the chair a little bit. The Gehova is being merciful to all humankind."

"I just happened to think of something, with this mercy thing."

"Mercy thing?"

"Well, you know. If humankind had no spirit, did humankind have a soul?"

"Back to 'the sixth day', and everything that moves on the earth there is a living soul. Remember that?"

"Hang on a sec; let me go back to the script."

"Take your time."

"Ah. Got it. So what is the difference between spirit and soul?"

"One of the best questions you have asked. The soul is humankind's moral and emotional nature of the mind. The spirit is that about humankind which is not material. Moral and emotional nature dies with the body and mind. The spirit is an essence that is immortal. The spirit lives forever."

"But the people about to die in the flood had no spirit. They could not live forever could they? So what happened to them?"

"The Gehova is not punishing. The Gehova gave them one hundred twenty years to repent. They did not, so would die. Well, those that are about to die in the flood will be taken care of. More about that later."

"Again with the more will be revealed."

"You got it. **These are the offspring of Noah—Noah was a righteous man, perfect in his walk with The Gehova;** meaning Noah was not corrupt even in the generation of corruption. He was not like his wicked contemporaries. **Noah walked with The Gehova. Noah begot three sons: Shem, Ham, and Japheth. The Earth was wicked before The Gehova and the Earth was filled with robbers. The Gehova saw the Earth was corrupted, for all of mankind was corrupt.** For all man was corrupt means my Nephilim had a part in it."

"Were the Nephilim killed along with humankind."

"No, they returned to the throne of Iawah with the other angels as their task on Earth had been accomplished."

"So, they were not punished?"

"No one is punished. There is no punishment. The punishment is the torment of the soul on Earth. Humankind punishes itself."

"When I write this, there are a lot of folks who will say it is an abomination. Do you realize the amount of people that believe in eternal damnation? Cast into the fires of hell forever. They'll stone me."

"Stoned again? Are you not being a little dramatic?"

"Yeah. But... well... I'm trying to make a point."

"The Earth is not the center of the universe, is it? Yet did not a host of people believe that for centuries. Even after it was proven the Earth revolved around the sun, the greatest institutions on the planet would not teach it for three centuries. I tell you these truths, the Earth is round, the Earth revolves around the sun, it is the center of no universe, and there is no punishment after death. What...again, I ask...would be the point?"

"Is it not a warning to keep people in line?"

"Again...has it worked? **The Gehova spoke to Noah, "The end has come, Earth is filled with wickedness. I am going to destroy them."** They were to be destroyed from the Earth. Nothing is said of anything befalling them after they are destroyed."

The Ark

"**Construct an Ark of gopher wood.** Do not even ask. **The Ark will have sections, pitch it inside and out so it will not leak. The size of the Ark will be—four hundred fifty feet in length, seventy-five feet in width and forty-five feet high. Make a window high on the side of the Ark, a foot and a half from the top deck. The Ark will be constructed with three decks and a large door will be put in the side.**"

"I can see why the window was so high on the ark. By the time the three floors were put into the ark it would be sitting low in the water."

"Wait, there is more."

"You mean putting all the animals on board."

"Yes, we will get to that shortly. **The Gehova spoke, "I am going to bring a flood on the Earth to destroy all living creatures on the ground and in the arc of the sky, everything that is in the Earth will die.""**

"In the Earth? I don't get that."

"Remember the face of the Earth we talked about. Everything that is in the Earth, applies as well here. Humankind was created from the Earth. So, it is humankind that will be destroyed. Only Noah and his family will survive. All the animals will be drowned except those that Noah brings onto the Ark and sea creatures."

"I don't quite follow you here."

"Let me go on a little further. I think you will be able to form your question from the next few verses. **The Gehova spoke, "My covenant will be good with you, and you will enter the Ark—you**

and your family. All that is alive, two of each bring into the Ark so that they may live with you, male and female. Each bird, and each animal, and the creatures that crawl on the ground, two of every kind will you keep alive.""

"I have several points I would like clarified."

"I thought you might."

"I realize that two of each would be put on the Ark. But the Ark is setting low in the water and two elephants, two rhinos and two hippos would put it under."

"'"Each bird, each animal and each crawling creature is the lineage of species. All cats lineage is from the saber-toothed cat, each dog from the wolf, each horse or hippo from the whale."

"Whales."

"The largest member of the horse family. The same is true of bird species and reptiles. Two snakes to begin the lineage to all snakes."

"That sure trims down the amount of animals on the Ark."

"Precisely. You have something else?"

"The animals, all living creatures, were created from the Earth as was man. Is it that man had no more soul, mind and body than the other creatures? The creatures had a soul? How can an animal have emotions and morals?"

"I was wondering when you would be getting around to this. Good time to discuss it. Have you ever seen an immoral animal? Have you ever seen an animal with emotions beyond instinct? Animals were given a soul, but do not have free will. That is the difference between humankind and animals. Humans have free will to emote and to be moral or not. Animals did not touch the fruit of the tree of the knowledge of good and bad. Animals have a soul given them by The Gehova. They have not been given a spirit, just as humankind has not."

"Will animals ever be given a spirit?"

"Yes. **Gather the fruits and grains of the Earth and use it for food for your family and all creatures on the Ark. Noah did everything that The Gehova instructed him.**"

"Noah gathered food for all on the Ark, yet he did not know how long the flood would last."

"Yes. And Noah did not have much time to do it."

"Why did they need food at all? We will be here a fortnight and I will not need food."

"I could give you a trite answer, such as, well The Gehova just wanted it that way. And of course that would be correct. The Gehova was testing Noah throughout the time of the preparation for the flood. Noah did everything to the letter that The Gehova instructed. Humankind takes care of the animals. From the beginning, it was humankind that was charged to name and rule over the animals. Noah and his family were to take care of the livestock. It was Iawah's wish from the fifth day. Throughout the script, there is lesson after lesson of The Gehova instructing humankind to do The Gehova's will."

"And then there are all those that did not do The Gehova's will."

"Indeed. **The Gehova said to Noah, "Go into the Ark, you and all your family, you have been righteous in this generation and will be saved. Every proper animal take seven pairs, a male and a female, and those animals that are not proper take only two, a male and a female.""**

"I take it is the proper, the kosher animals, that are of seven pairs."

"Very good, Sal."

""Of the proper birds take seven pairs, they will keep the seed alive on the Earth.""

"To pollinate?"

"Correct.**...in seven days I will send rain for forty days and forty nights and the death of all existence will begin, all the creatures I have given life on the Earth and in the arc of the sky, I will take them. Noah did everything that The Gehova instructed him to do.**"

"Do you ever wonder what would have occurred if Noah would not have done as instructed?"

"The Gehova told Noah that he was to survive. It may have been that survival instinct that made Noah abide in The Gehova. It may have been just that Noah was a righteous man and did his best to the good. Noah was given free will and used that will to become an upright and moral man. It was also that survival instinct that brought humankind to this brink of destruction. In sixteen hundred fifty-six years, humankind became so violent, such robbers, so immoral, that the species, if you will, had to be wiped out and humankind started all over again. The Gehova did this to save the species. I am sounding scientific, I know, but the survival of the species was the motivation behind the flood. Humankind would have wiped out their own species with war and murder and crime."

"Did not the Nephilim contribute to the downfall?"

"They did, in that humankind turned its back on the spiritual life offered by my angels. They chose instead to consort with them. Free will, again."

"So, the Nephilim were not responsible for the spirits of humankind. Your angels merely offered it. It was up to humankind to recognize the need for it?"

"And they did not. Humankind had the free will to accept it or not and they turned their back on it."

"Could they have avoided it...the flood?"

"No. It was the nature of humankind...violence...robbery... war..."

"Essentially, The Gehova just had enough of it."

"Correct. **When the flood began Noah was six hundred years old. Noah and his family went into the Ark as the flood waters were about to pour from the arc of the sky. Of the proper animals and birds Noah had seven pairs and of the improper animals and birds Noah had a pair just as The Gehova had instructed. All the creatures followed Noah and his family into the Ark. After seven days the flooding began.**

On the seventeenth day of the second month of the six

hundredth year of Noah's life the flood began... You want to say something?"

"Okay. This sounds like this is right out of the Gregorian calendar. The days of the month the second month on the seventeenth day of the month, what gives?"

"This was written so that when man calculated time, the time could be found by going forward. The times of the day, the days, months and years were always there—man just had to discover the calendar."

"I see."

"**...the waters from the Earth spilled over...** This shows that the water welled up from the seas as well as from the sky... **and the rain fell from the arc of the sky. It rained forty days and forty nights.**

Noah came with Shem, Ham, and Japheth and their wives and went into the Ark—and with them went all creatures of the ground and the arc of the sky. They went into the Ark with Noah two by two, a pair and seven pairs, a male and a female as The Gehova had instructed and The Gehova closed the door on Iawah's behalf."

"Closed the door on Iawah's behalf. Did The Gehova close it on Iawah's behalf or was it shut on Noah's behalf?"

"On Noah's behalf as Noah fulfilled all the instructions of The Gehova. The Gehova closed the door as the final act of saving humankind on the earth. It was the period at the end of the sentence of humankind. The Gehova closed in the righteous and shut out the wicked. In so doing, The Gehova also closed the door on Iawah's behalf."

"I am also amazed that the beasts got along with the domesticated animals. The saber-toothed cat with the cattle. The wolves with the rabbits."

"In those times, the animals, all living creatures, lived on vegetation."

"Everyone... all the animals... vegetarians?"

"Before the flood, yes. The Gehova had never given to Adam, Eve and their progeny permission to eat meat. It is when permission to eat meat is given to all living creatures that the beast and the domestic animals are no longer in accord. But we are getting way ahead."

The Waters Strengthened

"After forty days of rain the flood was so great the Ark lifted from the Earth. The Ark started to drift on the surface. The oceans under the arc of the sky were all one. Every living creature on the Earth and under the arc of the sky along with mankind had expired."

"Only that which lived on the earth and flew. Nothing in the waters was killed. Fish and whales survived?"

"Yes. **All the creatures of the Earth and skies died. The Gehova took their lives. All died except for Noah and his family."**

"We were talking about death without spirit. Does one who dies without spirit have an existence after the physical act of dying?"

"Noah did not yet have a spirit. If he would have died before acquiring a spirit he would have returned to dust as did all those taken in the flood."

"Their souls did not survive?"

"Remember the soul is the morals and emotions of humankind, distinct from the spirit, the soul does not survive death. Humankind had a body and a mind. And in the mind abides the soul. The knowledge of good and bad. But I tell you this, those that died in the flood and before the flood were given a spirit at the time of death and went on to the great reward of being angels of the third tier known as the angels of the principalities."

"They became angels. That seems like a reward for being wicked."

"Being wicked and being given a spirit gave them the opportunity to envision that which is not wicked. In the absence of wickedness the principalities could not appreciate that which was not wicked. But with wickedness in their experience, they were able to understand that which is magnificent. They were able to understand Iawah and all that is good. Iawah does not punish."

"What of the Nephilim?"

"My Nephilim returned to the fold."

"What level...what did you call it?

"Tier."

"Into what tier do the Nephilim fall?" You are in the top tier."

"You can relate to angels in tiers, hierarchies or as we like to call ourselves, in choirs. The first choir..."

"Choirs because angels sing praises to Iawah."

"Sal, you surprise me. Very good. Yes, that is exactly why the tiers are called choirs. In the first choirs are the Seraphim, then the Cherubim and then Thrones. I am in the same choir as the angel guarding the Garden of Eden. The angel is still at the passageway with a flaming sword in hand. The second tier or choir is first the Dominions, second the Virtues and last the Powers. The third choir holds Principalities, our Nephilim, then Archangels and Angels. It was in the Choir of Angels that all those who died before the flood were placed."

"Sounds like ranks in the army."

"A bit like that. To give you an example. Whenever a struggle exists between good and bad, the angels of the Choir of Powers become involved. The Choir of Cherubim are angels of vast knowledge and are records keepers."

"Of what do they keep records?"

"Of many things so that others will know. How do you think all that has been learned has been learned?"

"From angels?"

"Everything."

"Yes, everything."

"The flood got stronger for a hundred fifty days."

"I don't understand. It rained for forty days and nights. How is it the flood got stronger?"

"It not only rained, but the water welled-up from the springs in the ground. The rains stopped after forty days, but the springs kept welling. There is a significance to the number forty."

"What is that?"

"The number four represents unlimited freedom and zero is the capacity for action that is unlimited."

"Freedom and capacity for unlimited action."

"It is telling us that the flood is a spiritual wash. A wiping of the slate. Cleaned of all that is the knowledge of only that which is bad. To know that which is good and bad one must experience each. The flood is the true opening of the eyes. The flood is the true experience of the knowledge of the tree of good and bad."

"So, it was not until this time, the time of the flood, that humankind was given the knowledge of good and bad. So, why not when Adam and Eve touched the fruit ate the fruit?"

"They gained the knowledge of that which was of the tree. But all they did was know, not experience. The knowledge of good and bad is only brought about by experiences each with the other."

"I think I got it. They had not known either good or bad, so could not experience that which was the other. They knew not good, so couldn't experience bad and vice versa."

"And that is why they were forced from the garden. They preempted the knowing. They did not know knowing. To, know knowing, is no good if you do not know not knowing."

"I think I am getting this. I really do. Adam and Eve knew not and because they knew not they could not know. And because they did not know, they did not know that they did not know. This is all very round about."

"Not really. Look at it this way. If one does, not know, then one does, not know, and one does not, know. Adam and Eve experienced neither. So they knew not of either the knowing or not knowing of experience. Sure, they gained the knowledge of good and bad, but could experience neither. In essence, Adam and Eve were out of their minds. Not in the sense we normally attribute that statement. They had thoughts but only limited as their minds were freshly developed. They knew not."

"So, they didn't know much of anything?"

"That is why humankind did not know good and bad. Humankind only did what was necessary to survive, just as an animal wanting to survive. Humankind did not know bad from good and thus could not experience that which was not bad, good."

"Got it. Whew. So, now, through the flood comes the true knowledge of good and bad?"

"Yes. **Iawah remembered Noah and his family and all the creatures that were with him in the Ark,**"

"Now, we have gone full circle. From Iawah to The Gehova to Iawah. Iawah of the thought and idea. It is as if all is being created anew."

"True. Things are being created anew. **Iawah caused a spirit to pass over the Earth and the waters started to recede.**"

"Is this the spirit... the spirit given humankind?"

"It is the beginning of the responsibility of spirit given each of you."

"There is that word, responsibility, again."

"Think of it this way. Are you not responsible for your actions, your body, your thoughts...you get my drift?"

"So, now we are responsible for our spiritual... ah... what, development?"

"Precisely. **The fountains stopped flooding and the springs no longer welled up. For a hundred fifty days the water receded.**"

"The waters receded for one hundred fifty days as well. The streams and springs receded."

"The water from the rains on the surface began to

evaporate. The Ark settled on the mountains of Ararat on the seventeenth day of the seventh month."

"Turkey?"

"No, Armenia. Mount Ararat was named after the story of the flood. It is the mountains of Ararat, not Mount Ararat. **On the first day of the tenth month the waters had receded and the tops of the mountains were visible."**

Return the Dove, Nevermore

"**At the end of forty days, Noah opened the window of the Ark. He sent out the raven. The raven kept flying out and returning to the Ark.** Noah was testing the air to see if the air was too moist for the raven to fly. It was, as the raven kept circling and coming back. **Noah sent out a dove to see if the waters had receded. The dove could find nowhere to land and it too returned to the Ark. Noah put out his arm and the dove landed on it and he took the dove into the Ark. Noah waited another seven days and sent the dove out again. That evening the dove came back with an olive branch in its beak. The dove had plucked it from a tree.** When the dove brought back the branch, the symbol was that 'better a bitter leaf from The Gehova's hand than the sweetness of honey from the hand of humankind'. **After seven days Noah sent out the dove again and the dove did not return.** The number seven is symbolic. Seven represents fullness. It is the time taken for the creation, the six days and the day of rest. It is now that the Ark has come to rest. The tribulation of the flood has come to rest. And from that came the evolution and the fulfilling of that which was spiritual for the natural man."

"But we're still waiting for Shem?"

"We are. **On the first month of the six hundredth year, the waters dried. Noah celebrated as he took the cover from the Ark. The Earth had dried and on the twenty-seventh day of the second month the Earth was totally dried.** Here, the number six hundred represents spiritual unfolding. We are going to be getting into the unfolding of body, mind and spirit in a way that will be shown you by the begots of Ham, Japheth and Shem. But, more of that later."

A Bow from the Clouds

"**The Gehova spoke to Noah.** In the last chapter Iawah used the name The Gehova, The Gehova of the concept, when The Gehova told Noah the Ark would save him and closed the Ark. The Gehova, or Iawah is used here as it is The Gehova who dominates nature. The Gehova in this context means the mighty one who wields authority over the beings above and below."

"The Gehova wields?"

"If your mother loves you, and corrects you, and protects you, are these three different mothers? As with The Gehova, The Gehova plays many roles."

"Why then is The Gehova in this context referred to as The Gehova who wields? What does The Gehova wield?"

"Remember me telling you that Iawah is not punishing. The wielding of The Gehova is The Gehova's judgment of The Gehova. The Gehova judges The Gehova not humankind."

"Oh, really?"

"Stay with me. **Leave the Ark, you and your family. Take all the creatures in the Ark with you.** Take all the creatures means tell them to leave of their own accord as opposed to force them out if they refused to leave. **Let these creatures replenish the Earth. Noah took his family and all the creatures, and they came out of the Ark.**"

"**Noah built an alter to Iawah.** You see here that it was to the merciful Iawah that Noah built an alter. **And Noah took the proper animals and the proper birds and affirmed a burnt offering on the altar. The Gehova smelled the offering and was very**

pleased. What is pleasing to The Gehova was not the smell of the burning flesh but the act pleased The Gehova. This is also the first time an animal was killed by humankind. This is the first rendering of flesh. It was done to honor Gehova. It was not done for humankind's selfish reason. And before you ask, Abel brought the best of the flock. Abel killed none of the flock. **The Gehova spoke, "I will no longer curse the Earth because of man. Man's heart was evil from the first creation. I have taken the life of all creatures that live on the Earth and in the arc of the sky. From now on all beasts will fear man and the birds of the arc of the sky will fear man. But I will no longer take from the Earth all living creatures as long as there are days on the Earth."** This is where The Gehova judges The Gehova. In so doing, The Gehova will not wipe out humankind again. What The Gehova has done is in the past. Humankind must now live with evil in its heart as a condition of being. Humankind now has the full knowledge of good and bad and beyond that the knowledge of evil. These are taken from the tree by Adam, Eve and the serpent. The knowledge will always be with us as will the serpent and yes the serpent survived the flood. As long as there are days on the Earth The Gehova promises."

"I interpret this as the days of the Earth are numbered."

"One could come to that conclusion. **The days of the Earth, the spring and autumn, heat and cold, summer and winter, daytime and nighttime, will never cease.**"

"All the days of the Earth, huh...one wonders how fast we are on that path. Do you think The Gehova will destroy the Earth or humankind will?"

"That is up to humankind is it not? But The Gehova promised not to."

"Many believe in a great tribulation, out of our hands."

"That's nice."

"Wait a minute. It is humankind that will destroy the Earth. The Gehova promised to never wipe out or smite humankind again. 'We see the enemy and it is us', as the saying goes."

"So, what does that do to your tribulation story? When we first talked about humankind's spiritual responsibility...that humankind would someday have that responsibility, the spirit within us. Would we be delighted in the spirit or would a dark pall fall over us as our spirits became depressed? The greatest responsibility with which we have been tasked is to be responsible to the likeness of The Gehova. Morals and emotions of the soul and the light of The Gehova in the spirit is what is humankind like none other."

"This is the most emotional you have become during our interview. Why?"

"It grieves me to hear of The Gehova's tribulation. And in such a way as to think humankind cannot control its own destiny. You can, Sal, you can. Let us continue. **The Gehova spoke to Noah saying, "Fill the land with your progeny. All animals and birds and ocean creatures will fear you."** This next verse gives humankind the right to eat meat. Until this day humankind, all of humankind were vegetarians. **All the Earth's living creatures will be food for you. The same as the vegetation was before the flood. Of the blood you will not drink.** This could really be used as the first rule of koshering; the meat had to be drained of the blood. Blood was of the soul and not to be taken in the body."

"That sort of leaves a lot of dishes out of the picture...rare steak, blood pudding."

"This is all new to Noah and his family but to their progeny these are the conditions of humankind. There is more. And this is another interpretation. Humankind shall not eat humankind. Rather stark, do you not think?"

"Rather."

"Your soul's blood I will demand in death, and of every creature I will demand it, for every man I will demand his spirit. Of all things living will come death. The body and the soul shall perish on the earth. Only the spirit shall live in eternity. **Man was made in the image of The Gehova and should he spill the blood of a**

brother in the same way his blood will be spilt. This can be said to be the first law. But, as you read this, you see that it is at the hand of humankind that the murderer shall suffer. Killing is the taking away of the image of The Gehova. **Now, fill the Earth with your progeny.** This is another instruction, to beget children. **The Gehova spoke to Noah and his family saying "I establish my covenant with you, and with all living creatures that departed the Ark, and with all the creatures of the ocean. My covenant will be confirmed with you. Never again will I wipe out humankind by floods or fires or cold. Never again will I destroy the Earth."** This is where the tribulation buffs use fire as the second destruction of the earth. But that is just it…"

"The Gehova did not destroy the earth. And now promises not to do so. The Gehova destroyed the living things on it save Noah and his family."

"Very good. That was the point I was about to make. **The Gehova spoke to Noah and his family, "I will give a sign to you and to all the creatures of the Earth and of the arc of the sky and of the ocean. This sign shall be a rainbow from the clouds and every time you look upon a rainbow will be an affirmation of this covenant. By the rainbows do I promise you that never again will I destroy any man nor creature on Earth."** And this brings us to the end of the flood."

My Three Sons

"**Noah's sons,** the consciousness, **who were with him in the Ark were Shem,** meaning renowned spirit mind; **Ham,** meaning hot, body mind; **and Japheth,** meaning extended and wide, the intellect. **Ham begot Canaan**, a fourth plane, visible flesh. Canaan is important to the understanding of the progeny of Ham. **The progeny of the sons of Noah were spread throughout the world.**"

"The Canaan lineage is different from the lineage of Japheth and Shem. How?"

"The lineage from Canaan resulted in the knowledge of good and bad that influences humankind to this very day. As you will read, Noah is degraded. That degradation serves to demonstrate that even the loftiest of people can lose control and bring shame upon themselves. **Noah corrupted himself by planting a vineyard. He drank the wine and became drunk, he unclothed himself in his tent. Ham, the father of Canaan, saw his father and told his brothers. Japheth and Shem covered themselves with a garment and walked backwards into the tent and covered their father's nakedness. Neither Japhteh nor Shem saw their father's nakedness. Noah slept off his wine and knew what Ham had done. But instead of cursing Ham, Noah cursed Canaan and said that Canaan would be a slave to his brothers for all his days.**""

"Isn't this used to give credence to the belief that the lineage of Ham is black, a negro, and it is this curse that brought them into slavery?"

"Belief in something for a long enough period of time can give credence to anything if enough people take it as fact. Newton's laws are taken as fact, although disproved. People believe Einstein's theories are proven although they are just that, theories. They have been on the books so long people take the theories as fact. It was convenient for slave owners to believe that the lineage of Ham had an everlasting curse on them. What is worse is that slaves were lead to believe it. No, the curse is the reaffirming of the knowledge of good and bad. The meaning is that humankind, still and forever, will be burdened by that knowledge. Humankind will suffer on Earth because of it. **Noah spoke, "Let this be a blessing to The Gehova, The Gehova of Shem; and let Canaan be a slave."** We attribute to Canaan the knowledge that without bad we cannot experience good. Without evil we cannot experience that which is magnificent. Also, you notice that Noah blessed The Gehova, The Gehova of Shem. The Gehova is the spiritual lineage that begins with Shem. **Noah spoke to Jepheth, "Let The Gehova extend to you, and Canaan is your slave."** All roads are starting to lead to Shem. From Shem comes the spirit."

"Are you saying that from Shem will come the spirit to humankind? Humankind is about to experience spirituality?"

"And the responsibility for it. The magnificence of The Gehova or the curse of Canaan. Humankind now has total free will. Over sixteen hundred fifty-six years of humankind lost to spirit because of Adam and Eve. **Noah lived for three hundred fifty years after the Flood. Noah died after living nine hundred fifty years.**

"Wasn't there a limitation, on humankind, one hundred twenty years?"

"That was before the flood and allowed humankind to live one hundred twenty years to correct their sins. Humankind did not and the flood, the spiritual wash, was brought upon them."

"Spiritual wash. The flood. I understand that. Spiritual wash."

Races

"As we go through the begots after the flood you will see the conditions of the mind, body and spirit. Each attributed to the lineage of the sons of Noah. With each name I shall describe the condition. Note that some of the conditions are not positive, yet with the spirit all save one are positive. **These are the progeny of the sons of Noah: Shem,** meaning renowned, that which is spiritual. **Ham** meaning blackened. Ham represents the physical **and Japheth,** meaning the intellect, the mental and the soul in humankind, the unfolding. **The sons of Japheth were Gomer,** perfected; **Magog,** extension; **Madai,** capacity; **Javan,** deception; **Tubal,** triumphal; **Meshech,** deducing; **and Tiras,** imagination. **The sons of Gomer were Ashkenaz,** overthrowing confusion and also, fire that spreads. It is Ashkenaz that is the progenitor of the occidental race. In English, Ashkenaz means German; **Riphath,** pardon; **and Togarmah,** centralizing energy. **The sons of Javan were Elishah,** uprightness of The Gehova; **the Kittim,** this refers to the people of Kittim, meaning outsiders; **and the Dodanim,** the peoples of Dodanim, confederates. **Each were islands separated by languages, and families, in their nations.**"

"Was not the entire world of one language? Do we not see that in the story of the tower of Babel?"

"We will see that the people of Babel were of one language before the end of the begots."

"As in separated here, according to language?"

"Exactly. **The sons of Ham,** body; **were Cush,** burned, it is here that the negro peoples have their lineage; **Misraim,** bondage; **Put,** suffocation; **and Canaan**, inferior. **The sons of Cush,** burned; **were Seba,** intoxicated; **Havilah,** struggle of life; **Sabtah,** motion; **Raamah,** tremble; **and Sabteca,** intensified intoxication. **The sons of Raamah,** tremble; were **Sheba,** rest; **and Dedan,** physical attraction.

"So we have Ashkenaz, occidental, and Ham, negro."

"Two of the three races."

"Three races."

"There are only three."

"Oh, really."

"**Cush,** burned; **begot Nimrod,** ruling will. **He was the first to be a mighty man on Earth. He was a mighty hunter blessed by The Gehova; therefore it is said: Like Nimrod a mighty hunter before The Gehova. The beginning of his kingdom was Babel,** chaos of speech; **Erech,** slack; **Accad,** fortitude; and **Calneh,** completed; **in the land of Shinar,** rivers. A**sher,** level, from the lineage of Cush; **built Nineveh,** animal forces in humankind's body; **Rehovoth-ir,** forums; **Calah,** ancient; **and Resen,** power from above; **between Nineveh and Calah, the great city. And Mizraim,** bondage; **begot Ludim,** travails; **Anamim,** statues; **Lehabim,** passionate; **Naphtuhim,** hollow; **Pathrusim,** dust; **and Casluhim,** forgiveness; **whence the Philistines,** wanderers; **came from, and Caphtorim,** converted.

"The Philistines were negroes?"

"The lineage of Cush: **Canaan,** inferior; **begot Zidon,** hunter; **and Heth,** terror; **and the Jebusite,** profane; **the Amorite,** peoples of the mountains; **the Girgashite,** dense; **the Hivite,** wicked; **the Arkite,** carnal; **the Sinite,** hateful; **the Arvadite,** greed; **the Zemarite,** despot; **and the Hamathite,** confidence in material conditions. **The families of the Canaanites,** inferior peoples, **spread out. The Canaanite bounds extended from Zidon,** hunter; **toward Gerar,** camp; **and went as far as Gaza,** power; **toward Sodom,** hidden wiles; **Gomorrah,** oppressed; **Admah,** silent; **and Zeboiim,** plunder; **as far as Lasha,** actuated. **These are the progeny of Ham and these are the living places of their families.**

"Never, would I have figured out the names and their meanings. Knowing that sheds a whole new light upon the mind and body. Now, I guess we are going on to the spirit. The moment of truth."

"Yes. **Shem is in the name of all those that live on the other side.**"

"The other side? Do tell."

"Humankind did not have the spirit upon itself until now. It was in the hands of The Gehova. On the other side, **the brother of Japheth the elder. The sons of Shem,** names, in this case the name of The Gehova, the spirit of The Gehova) **were Elam,** eternal; **Asshur,** harmonious; **Arpachshad,** ruling star; **Lud,** creation; **and Aram,** exalted. **The sons of Aram were Uz,** formative; **Hul,** ecstasy; **Gether,** abundance; **and Mash,** harvest. **Arpachshad,** ruling star; **begot Shelah,** prayer; **and Shelah begot Eber,** grace. **Eber had two sons: The first was Peleg,** higher nature divided **for in his life the Earth was divided and the name of his brother was Joktan,** the life of the unfolding individual. **Joktan begot Almodad,** a measure, as in a measure of The Gehova; **Sheleph,** reaction; **Hazarmaveth,** place of death; **Jerah,** inspired; **Hadoram,** majesty; **Uzal,** divine going forth; **Diklah,** the ethereal; **Obal,** barren matter; **Abimael,** divine father; **Sheba,** rest; **Ophir,** purity; **Havilah,** struggle of life; **and Jobab,** wail of joy. **Joktan's sons lived away from Mesha,** freedom; **toward Sephar,** remembering; **the mountain to the east,** or the good mountain. **These are the progeny of Shem representing the conditions of the spirit.**"

"Hazarmaveth, meaning place of death."

"That was the one I told you about. The only negative condition. **The families of Noah were separated by their nations.**"

"Was Shem oriental?"

"Yes. Very good. Thus giving us the three races, Ham, body, negro; Japheth, mind-soul, occidental; and Shem, spirit, oriental. And now humankind is fully responsible for the body, the mind, the soul and at last, the spirit."

"By their nations."

"We are about to get into the dispersion a little deeper."

Nimrod's Place

"A part of Nimrod's kingdom was the city of Babel. Separated by languages refers to the division of the tribes of the descendants of Ham, Japheth and Shem. It was the son of Cush that was given the great kingdom. The collapse of the tower of Babel came about before all the generations were complete and the timing is thus, that the languages were common, and the lineage of the three sons were together in one land until the begots were complete. The story of the Tower of Babel occurred prior to the end of the lineage as it is written. Therefore, the time line is correct in that: **The Earth was of one language and of one culture. It came to be that they traveled from the east into the land of Shinar and set up a dwelling there.**"

"If they migrated from the east were they not going from the good to the bad? Out of the east, the good, to elsewhere."

"Yes. **They said to one another, Let us create a furnace and make bricks. The bricks served as their stones for building, and the bitumen served them as their mortar. They spoke, "Let us build a city, and a tower ascending into the heavens, and let us be named a people that is not dispersed over the earth.""**

"Is this...do the people believe...do they believe that the sky, as referred to by The Gehova as the heavens, was really a place where they could come in contact with The Gehova?"

"This is where the heavens are referred to as a place of The Gehova. The sky above has nothing to do with the place where The Gehova resides. That thought is a product of a great misinterpretation of the creation of the heavens. Call it heaven, sky, that above the earth, arc of the sky, whatever. It has not a thing to do with the residence of The Gehova."

"Okay. Then where is it The Gehova resides?"

"In the eternal. You cannot get to where The Gehova is until you are taken from the body and mind and enveloped in the spirit."

"When I die?"

"Exactly. But you never die. Oh, you do as you see it. But until you leave your body and your mind you will not know the place of The Gehova. Earth, your world, is for experiencing that which is not magnificent, so you can know the magnificent. This is the premise of your quote at the beginning of our lesson. The reason we are having this discussion. The Gehova takes a dim view of the people of Babel wanting or believing that something so simple could allow them to know the intimacy and intricacy of The Gehova. **The Gehova looked at the city and the tower that the sons of man had built.**"

"Whoa. The sons of man, the Nephilim, your guys again?"

"You bet. Just as the with the flood, my guys, as you call them, were there to make sure of the dispersion."

"As the flood was called for?"

"It would never have happened without the sons of man, my guys, as you say. Fallen angels are responsible for a lot of that which is not magnificent. **The Gehova spoke, "They are of one people, one culture and one language, and they have built this tower!"** Note the emotion. **"Now I will stop them from building this abomination. Let us go down there,"** The Gehova is calling on the angels. **"and confuse their language that they may not interpret each other."**"

"Good angels fighting bad angels."

"I have no power over good angels."

"You are a bad angel. Sorry, I don't mean to call you bad. But angels, other angels, have power over you?"

"Oh, yes. I am the leader of the Nephilim. I was the first star to fall from the sky. I am the best of the worst."

"Well I'll be..."

"The Gehova dispersed them over the Earth; and the city was abandoned. It was there The Gehova confused the language of the Earth, and scattered them. There ends the lesson."

And with a nod of his head, Helel faded away. I was startled, not expecting him to leave. It felt like we had just gotten started and yet I knew he had given me the answers I needed for the unsolved quote I had held in my head for so long. When I looked up after picking-up my notes and scripts, I was in my own apartment, sitting on the sofa. Somewhat confused but not totally surprised, I was curious to know the time and day. Sure enough, when I looked at the digital clock in my bedroom, it had stopped when I had left. The appointment that the envoy had arranged for me. The clock began to run again as did all of the other clocks in my place. Helel had given me all that information in the time that he had stopped for me. I still had two week's vacation to put all that I had learned in a format that I could publish. When I returned to the living room, I saw the stack of papers that I had accumulated while taking notes with Helel. The papers were a brilliant, bright white. When I picked the stack up to begin my writing, I could feel what I had felt in Helel's apartment. I felt his presence. I reached in my pocket for the tape recorder. I clicked it on and the sound of Helel's voice was clear and loud. I had captured an angel on tape. Here was the proof that all that had happened to me was not just a dream or an imagination gone wild. But who would believe me? Helel had told me that only I would hear his voice on the tape recorder and only I would be able to see the papers I had collected. This meant that I was now faced with my toughest assignment as a reporter...to publish an article that my readers would understand 'If we have not discovered that which is not in us, that which is in us, cannot be found'. Although I had learned so much from Helel, as a reporter I knew I needed to answer new questions.

Having gone this far I was not going to let myself be diverted. I started to leaf through the bright, brilliant papers, in hopes of finding something that might go beyond the lessons of Helel. As expected, the text of our conversation...well...it was word for word. There was even a faded likeness of Helel on the last page...a watermark. And on the bottom was written, Arpachshad Anael PhD, CD. Who was that? I asked as I pulled the name up on my laptop? I looked back through the text, the script and found that Arpachshad meant ruling star. Anael popped up on the screen as an angel of creation. Had Helel given me a new piece to the puzzle.Finding this guy would be my next adventure.

Double A

With a name like Arpachshad Anael, meaning the creation angel of the ruling star, I tried to figure out where to start. If this was an angel, I felt confident in doing an interview, having interviewed Helel. However, in the angel books I had bought, none were listed with a PhD or CD. I had no idea what discipline the PhD was nor did I know what the CD stood for. Thinking the online might have more information, I went to my computer and just put in the name. Wham. Up came Arpachshad Anael, PhD, CD. The bio was posted beneath the cover of a book titled Earth Alone. Although no vitals were listed, it showed that Anael had studied and earned the PhD in Philosophy at the Ceely Institute and earned a Cosmology Doctorate, the CD, at UC-Bainbridge in the Aerospace Department. What an interesting combination. Anael had held a teaching position at UC-Bainbridge in California before apparently dropping off the radar in 2000. The last project noted in the clip about Anael's work was to study the heavens past the millennium. Anael argued before several scientific societies that the millennium began January 1, 2001. Which one would think required no argument. The book was listed in the fields of aerospace studies, creation studies, cosmology and science of parsec measures. I had to look up parsec so I clicked onto netopedya.com *and read 3.26 light years or 19.2 trillion miles. Good grief. I hoped I could understand Anael. I went on a book seller website and there was a copy of the book, used, for six bucks. I put it in the cart and read that it would be here in three days. On vacation now, I was going to relax until the rush-order of the book came through. Three days to continue the search as to where to find Anael.*

I pulled up everything from World Geo to New Jersey Science and found only a repeat of the bio and pictures of the book. No pictures of the author at all. So, I would have to wait a few days. By the name, I didn't know if I was going to be reading works of a man or a woman. I decided to pour myself into a story of the interview with Helel. I would write a feature story. I also laid out an outline for the book length story of the creation. I considered keeping it in the conversation format with the scrip as a guide. I would go through the script and edit it. I had a line on a publisher. They were familiar with my crime reporting and indicated that if I had anything feature length, to give them a call. But before I started all that I thought I would walk down to the corner and have a beer or two at Nick's.

Well, it didn't take three days. The three volume work was in my hands in two days. I looked at the inside flap and back—no picture. But the bio on the book said 'Arpachshad Anael is a renowned Cosmologist. Doctor Anael has taught and lectured in the United States and Europe and lives in King of Prussia, Pennsylvania'. Great. I thought. A stone's throw from Philadelphia. It was not even a long distance call. Sure enough there was a listing. I got a machine—"Hi, this is Double A, leave your name and number and I may call you back. And, Sal, the big bang had nothing to do with The Gehova's creating the Earth. I'll call you in the morning." It was a soft, soothing voice. At least I now knew Doctor Anael was a woman. But how did she know I was going to call? She had my name on her machine. Like with the envoy of Helel, my first reaction was to call her back and to ask how she knew I was looking for her and wanted to interview her. But as with the envoy, I knew I was going to go with the flow. As for the big bang comment, I had no idea what that was all about. I left my name and phone number and the reason I would like to talk with her, if she could fit me in her schedule.

I had gotten in from Nick's about one. I started reading Anael's books. Her writing was fascinating. About six thirty the phone rang. Although I had not expected a call back from Doctor Anael, especially so soon after me leaving my message, before I picked up the phone I knew it was Doctor Anael. I was ready, no fuzzy head for this. Again, with her soft voice, she asked that I not ask any questions over the phone and suggested that we meet the next day. It seems Anael was involved in a research project at Francis Polytechnic. If it was alright with me, how was a two thirty meeting in her office in the astronomy department and laboratory building. Although excited beyond words about the prospect of this interview, I calmly replied, "I'm looking forward to it."

I was on campus by twelve and went to the student union café, got a coffee and started framing my questions. First on my mind was why Helel guided me to Doctor Anael and what was their relationship. Next was the big bang question. I felt I was about to get into an interview that also required a script, so I brought Earth Alone along. With her PhD and CD, I hoped Anael talked in lay terms or it would be rough going. I thought that for an ice breaker, I'd ask about her ongoing work.

The time came for me to walk across campus to Anael's office. I was excited about the interview. What was the link to a fallen angel? Was Anael a member of the Nephilim? Sal, cool it. I had to talk to myself to get calmed down. This isn't a crime scene in north Philly. What have you got to worry about? My cell rang. "Sal I'm running a little late. Just go into the office and make yourself comfortable." Good, I would do that. Then it dawned on me I had never given Anael my cell number. This was getting eerie, a little mind blowing. I went into the conference room and sat down to go over my notes. It wasn't too long until I heard a door open in an adjacent room. A door at the end of the conference table was slightly ajar. "Hey," came the voice. "Come on in and have a seat." I scooped up my note pad and went into the office.

When I entered the room, I stopped in my tracks. I don't know what I was expecting, but before me stood a most stunning, gorgeous, six feet tall, brunette. She looked like she had just stepped out of Vogue. She was beautiful. As she came around the desk to shake my hand, she introduced herself in her soft, soothing voice. "Pleased to meet you Sal. I'm Doctor Anael, please call me Double A." I hoped I was not standing there with my mouth agape. When making arrangement for the interview, even though I knew she was a woman, I had assumed she would look like most of the professors I had in school. I had just assumed...something a reporter should not do. Lesson learned, again.

The Metaphor of Enoch

"I have my questions about the first days of creation. Do you mind following in that order?"

"Not at all. Please, have a seat. When did you conclude your interview with Helel?"

"I don't know. I came from the interview at the same time I started. Back to when I left my apartment. I guess you could say we stayed in the now."

"Good answer."

"Will we stay in the now for this interview, also?"

"I am afraid not. Time will move along into the future."

"I did not have a chance to read your book. I skimmed the chapter heads and framed a lot of my questions from it. I will try to read it as we go along, in the evenings."

"That will be fine, but it isn't necessary. All will be explained as we go along."

"How was the book received. Your explanation of the creation time-line, especially that? Did you catch any flack from religious groups?"

"Oh, you bet. I was nailed, as you say when you do a tough interview. I was nailed by at least one person at each of my book signings. But, each time when I asked them to frame their own time-line, all they could do is call me a blasphemer. They were nut cases mostly. I always felt that the most devout had to have the most proof. Yet, in every instance, the antagonists could offer no theory of their own. It seemed they just disagreed with everything I said. One group actually bought an ad in that other Philly paper reviewing my book. It was a horrible review—sales went up."

"Your name? Very unusual."

"I like it."

"You have to admit it is an eye catcher. Do many people know it is the creation angel of the ruling star?"

"That is how the interpretation comes about from the original tongue. You and Helel used The Ricci New Age Version. We will be on the same sheet of music, so to say."

"Good. My notes and questions are framed from the Ricci Version as a reference. So, tell me how did you come to be at Francis Poly?"

"I am a visiting researcher. I have a three year posting."

"Just to get a little background information. Where were you born?"

"I was not born. I came to be."

"Sort that out a little, if you please. After Helel, I am not easily shocked."

"Oh, I did not say that to shock you. It is merely a statement of truth. I have no parents and was not born to anyone. I am a creation of The Gehova."

"How many people have you told this to?"

"You, Sal, you are the first and only one."

"But how can you get a driver's license, get a student ID? I mean you have to negotiate a lot of government agencies to do the work you do, grants, clearances.?

"Okay."

"Okay. How do you do it?"

"I change positions a lot. Due to my features, which do not change, I give different information to suit my age, not age really, my physical being. As I change locations and positions, I change the information in my past records."

"How?"

"Yes, indeed, how?"

"Oh. Okay. This is one of the most tactless questions I have ever asked. Will you die?"

"No, I will be taken by The Gehova."

"When? Do you know?"

"No, that is the one true mystery."

"So, you just wish your background information to be changed and it happens?"

"It must be that way. I could not function otherwise."

"What about the book? It goes out of print after years. You don't age. People will know."

"There is no date on the book, no date of publication. And it is now out of print. As a matter of fact, there are several errors in the book. Things I have come to understand differently since the time I wrote it."

"I did notice that there was no date on it. Well, I am a little taken aback with this. This is as if you were Enoch. Enoch was born though, but did not die. It reads, he was taken by The Gehova."

"True, I know Enoch. More will be revealed."

"More will be revealed. Where have I heard that before?"

"Do tell. Have you got enough background information?"

"I think so. I am sure more questions will come to me tonight. Will you mind if I ask you about yourself as we go along?"

"Not at all."

"I am sure I will have questions about your not aging. That fascinates me. Have you ever...er...are you married?"

"No, and I have no children."

"Enoch did."

"That's nice."

"There we go. You and Helel must compare notes. That brings up a big question. Something that crossed my mind. Why me? I am sure that I am not the only one to ask that question...quote that quote."

"No, but you are the only one to ask it when it is time to discover the truth. The truth about the creation story. It is now time to meld science and the creation story. The world is ready for it. Beware, when you write this, you will be challenged. People won't throw stones at you, but you will take a lot of flack, so to say. Be prepared."

"I thought that way about the interview with Helel. Who will believe me?"

"Indeed who? You may be thought of as a madman. Were not those discoverers, who came before you, ridiculed, punished, and burned at the stake. How long was it taught that the earth was flat, though it was proven to be a sphere and not the center of the universe, but that Earth revolved around the sun? I will tell you—centuries. Why? Because humankind was not ready for the unveiling. To have one's eyes opened to new facts is difficult. Many will go to the truth kicking and screaming. You have been chosen to lead them there."

"I don't know if I am ready for this."

"Sure you are, or you would not have been chosen to be the one. You can take the heat. You will have the courage when the time comes. But what I will reveal to you is not a theory. You will see the science involved in the creation. You will be the first believer on the Earth. You will go forth and teach. By your written word the truth will be revealed. How do you like that, Sal, my man?"

"Whew."

"I think we have had a very good, getting to know each other, day. Let us pick this up tomorrow, at say, seven in the morning. Nah. Let's make it nine. Cross town traffic and all."

"More will be revealed."

Too Much Coffee

Six o'clock in the morning came around too fast. I had just finished reading the first volume of Doctor Anael's Earth Alone. Only one mention of The Gehova was in the three hundred fifteen pages of the book, The Gehova Did Not Create The Earth And The Big Bang At The Same Time was the chapter title. Earth Alone was a scientific treatment of the stars and the size and the magnitude of it all. I wrote down scores of notes. I was looking forward to the morning meeting. I still had some questions about her life on earth. It was true there was no date on the book, no copyright either. I was in the car by seven and on my way to the student union café. I knew I was going to need a gallon of coffee to get through the day. I didn't mind. I lived off of coffee when I was on a case. Crime does not punch a clock. I made it to Double A's office by nine. She was sitting at the conference table.

"Good morning, Sal."

"Crime does not punch a clock."

"Beg pardon?"

"Just writing in my notes. Notes for the transcript. If you don't mind I would like to record our interview."

"Oh, go right ahead. You have three cups of coffee."

"Yeah. I was up all night reading Earth Alone."

"Well?"

"I was surprised that it had only one topic. I was expecting a little of the creation story thrown in."

"Could you imagine what the scientific community would do to me if I stirred that can of worms?"

"So, you are going to let stirring the can of worms to me?"

"Yup."

"All because of the quote."

"Marcellus III. Do you have any questions about the books' publication?"

"Yes, I do. Why no copyright?"

"Did not need one. We only had one printing anyway. Also, I wanted the community to use the work in any way they wanted. I have a lot of figures that no doubt will be quoted. It is not important to me to be quoted. As I find sometimes, copyrights can retard the process of science. Also, I wanted no dates on it. Time line for me, don't you know."

"I get it. I have some other questions before we start into the deep stuff."

"Deep stuff?"

"Creation and science."

"I think you are going to love that. But go ahead with your questions."

"How long ago did you come to Earth?"

"I worked as a team member on the Manhattan Project in Chicago. Under another name. I had to create a history to get a clearance. That was a time."

"You worked on the atom bomb?"

"Sure did. I left the project in the late forties and disappeared until the late seventies. I worked on non-stable theory."

"Non-stable?"

"Yes. I worked in the field of expanding effects. That the 'entirety' was expanding all the time. From the very first millisecond the 'entirety' has been expanding."

"Entirety. Do you mean the universe?"

"The term universe or universal means different things to lay-persons as well as scientists. That is why, throughout the book I referred to the all, the everything in space, as the 'entirety'. All the stars, planets, galaxies, and all the space in between is the 'entirety'. A universe to some people means our solar system, or the Milky Way. The Milky Way is but one galaxy in the trillions of galaxies out there. 'Entirety'."

"I always thought of it as our universe, not the universe. But I have a few other questions about your agelessness. Does that not cause a great problem, even moving every few years?"

"Not really. All my research in this, my present self, is with students. And they all move on after a few years. Also, I only work in research. The grants dry up and the projects change, as do the people. I have no lasting friendships or relationships. I am here for one reason."

"And that is?"

"I am here to move you from a crime reporter to an important scientific writer. Not to say that crime reporting is not important. But, you have to admit that the clarifying of the creation of all things Earthly by The Gehova and the development of this rock we call home is going to have an impact on two communities."

"And from both I will catch flack. Let's go back a bit. You worked on the first atom bomb. How did you feel about blowing cities to smithereens? I mean it was not The Gehova like endeavor."

"The same way I feel about the work I am doing now. Science."

"Which is?"

"The measuring of the 'entirety'."

"What is that exactly?"

"I go from a known point. I start with the age of stars, the solar systems in which they are the center, the galaxies in which they are captured, in gravity that is, and the space between these entities of the 'entirety'."

"The age. And that allows you to measure distance?"

"Yes. We, the scientific community, have an idea of how old the entities of the 'entirety' are by the distance between them. If you know the age you know the distance and if you know the distance you know the age. It is like the way we measure the time of the Earth's crust. We can tell the ages of the layers of the crust by the sediment and the carbon dating of the fossilized matter. Thus, the layers tell us the age of the fossils and the fossils tell us the age of the layers. More of this later. What I am doing now is to define the 'entirety' as far as we can measure it. The 'entirety' going beyond what we can see, measure, compute with any accuracy. My search is for the depth of the 'entirety'. Is there an edge? Is there a boundary? If so, what is the 'entirety' contained in? Is there a boundary for it all or only a portion? And if the 'entirety' has a boundary, what then? You know there are those that have driven themselves mad over these questions?"

"I have no doubt. There is one question I did not put in my notes, but it has just come to me now. You said that The Gehova is not the big bang."

"The understanding of The Gehova has a lot to do with the understanding of the Earth. The creation story you studied with Helel has to do with what?"

"The creation of the 'entirety'."

"Oh, contraire. The study of the creation story. Let's not call it a story. The study of the creation was of the creation of the Earth, was it not?"

"Well, there was the moon and the stars and the sun."

"Okay. But on a day The Gehova created the light and, day and night. But it was not until another day that the sun the moon and the stars came to be by the lifting of the pall over the Earth. Why is that?"

"I missed that. I completely missed that when I was with Helel."

"No, not really. You were studying the creation. Now, we are studying the 'entirety'. The great all; the all of everything. The creation is about the Earth, only Earth."

"We are going to study the 'entirety' to get to the creation? The creation of the Earth."

"To understand the creation, we have to look into that which was created before the Earth. But before that, let's clear up the question."

"Did you measure the force of the atom? What did you do on the Manhattan Project? Measure? Measure parsecs?"

"Measure. That is a good term for what I did. I was not a very big cog in the wheel. I transcribed notes and cataloged findings. It was a ground level experience."

"Which raises another question. Why not just have it all happen? Just float out to the edge of the 'entirety' and see for yourself?"

"Oh, but I am incarnate. I am bound to the Earth. I can't go about willy-nilly and discover what I wish. I, like Helel, am bound to the Earth."

"Yes, but, we have astronauts going into space. Why can't you?"

"Going to the moon and back is not all that much space. Staying within the orbit of Earth is but a small step. A very small step."

"Excuse me. I am getting a little dopey. Even the coffee can't stop the yawns."

"Look. I have some papers to read. It'll take me the rest of the day. So, why don't you go home, get some rest, and we can resume this tomorrow. Nine?"

"Nine sounds fine. Thanks. See you in the morning."

Drab and Dreary

To prepare myself for next morning's meeting, I reread the creation from the first verse of Genesis chapter one, to the end of the sixth day. I wanted to prepare for the science. The science of the 'entirety' as we now referred to the universe, all that is, and all that is not. I could have delved more deeply into the science of it all but chose not to. I wanted to hear it all from Arpachshad. Doctor Anael's book Earth Alone was a standalone treatment of the creation of 'entirety'. It was so radically different from anything I had ever read. It was in deep scientific terms. I could not grasp some of the science. The measurements were beyond me, the millions of light years, the parsecs of distances. I knew that the measurements had to be put in lay terms. If I did not understand a parsec is 31 trillion km or 19 trillion miles or 3.26 light years, I knew my readers would not understand. Even though Doctor Anael measures in parsecs, in the morning meeting, I was going to ask her to translate the measurements into millions, billions and trillions.

Having been down this path with Helel, to learn more about the quote I wanted to unravel it with Doctor Anael. After our conversation the previous day, I was humbled that I had been chosen to be the messenger. For me, this was not my usual tough guy experience of crime reporting. It was deep, wide, high and meaningful. As the time approached for our morning interview, my enthusiasm was at an all time high. What was I going to discover? What was going to manifest from the meeting with Helel and the writings of Doctor Anael?

"I see you are making this a one cup morning. How was your evening?"

"Very good. I reread the creation."

"Good idea. And what do you believe we are about to study? I am curious."

"Space, the final frontier."

"Wise guy."

"No. I deal with them on my regular beat."

"Very good. But space is not it for today. We are going back to a day. So, I am glad you reviewed the creation."

"I am ready professor. Lead on."

"If I said to you that the creation was drab and dreary, what would be your first thought?"

"That is was a rainy day in autumn."

"Okay. Now, if I say to you, it became drab and dreary, what would be your first thought?"

"It would still bring up the same thought... rainy, overcast. The only difference is, was versus became. But the meaning is essentially the same."

"Essentially, essentially the same. Why not exactly the same?"

"If you ask the question with was, it is past tense. If you ask the question with became, it could be past tense or present tense. It depends upon the context."

"Stick with me now as this gets very subtle."

"Alright."

"It was is indeed past tense, but using was only tells of the event, as in drab and dreary, in a singular context. It issues no thought as to the condition before the drab and dreary. By merely stating it was gives only the condition of drab and dreary."

"I think I am with you. Please. Continue."

"The was was, so to say. You do not think of the condition before it was. Now, let us go to became. Using became in the past tense allows the understanding that there was an event before it became drab and dreary. It may have been bright and warm."

"I see what you mean."

"Or, before it became drab and dreary it was full of fire and dust, then it became drab and dreary. Drab and dreary now becomes a better condition than when it was not drab and dreary, before it was drab and dreary. Even using the condition of drab and dreary, in the present tense still gives the message that there was something before drab and dreary, that it became drab and dreary."

"As in, today it became drab and dreary. Yesterday, it was full of fire and dust."

"Exactly. The use of the word became is the key, yet was and became in the past tense mean exactly the same thing. Do they not?"

"Yes, they do."

"What I am getting to here is something I want you to keep in mind as we go through the cosmos."

"We will be getting back to this?"

"We will refer back to this as we move along. But allow me to continue a bit further. In the every first verse of Genesis, it is written 'In the beginning of Iawah's creation—when the Earth was void, with nighttime on the surface of the deep'. Remember?"

"Yes."

"Well, there is that word was. Our was signifies the past tense, therefore we could then determine that the Earth found itself in a condition of void with nighttime. Keep in mind that the Earth was."

"The Earth was already there. I did not catch that either. So, the Earth was in a condition of was; the Earth was."

"Now, let me compound the lesson a little more. The word was in the original tongue is hayah. The very same word is used for..."

"Became... sorry to interrupt."

"Not at all. Go on.

"So, with the connotation of was the same as became in this context... the Earth was something before void with nighttime. The Earth became void with nighttime."

"Exactly. The Earth became void with nighttime."

"Signifying that there was something, some condition that the Earth was in before that. Something before void with nighttime."

"This is a very cryptic point in our study of the creation. I want you to keep this in mind as we search the stars over the next few days. Was as became. We will return to this when the time is right."

"Are we done for the day?"

"I am afraid so. I have to attend a luncheon and presentation. Back to the parsecs, don't you know?"

"Nine tomorrow?"

"Yes, and do you mind working over the weekend?"

"Not at all. Do you have anything for me to study?"

"You may want to go back over the first four days."

"Very subtle there, also. Helel and I touched on that."

"So, my friend. Do not labor over this too much. We will get to it all in due time. More will be..."

"Revealed. See you tomorrow."

U.F.O.s

"When you write, do you write to music?"

"At home I do. In the office, all you hear is the click of keyboards. Rather cramped."

"What kind of music?"

"Theme music from crime shows, some of the old ones: themes from 'Mike Hammer', theme from 'Peter Gun', stuff like the 'Streets of San Francisco'. Yeah, cop shows. How about you: do you listen to anything special?"

"I do much of the same thing from space shows, 'Star Trek'; 'Close Encounters';...you know."

"Do you believe UFOs have ever landed on Earth?"

"Not really."

"Based on science?"

"Yes, of course. It just seems so improbable, so impossible."

"Do go on. Oh, and if you are going to give me distances, please do so in kilometers or miles. I think I will understand it better and for my readers, too."

"I was planning on that. I only use parsecs in the community."

"I'm ready for the tough stuff."

"Do you believe there are other planets that sustain life?"

"Yes, I do."

"And what do you base that opinion on?"

"It just seems that with all the thousands of planets out there, others have to sustain life."

"Trillions. Trillions of stars and planets."

"Trillions?"

"Yes. Trillions of stars in our galaxy alone. The Milky Way is but one of an uncountable amount of galaxies. When I say uncountable, I mean in the trillions, also."

"This is almost too much to comprehend."

"Not if you set your mind to the magnitude of it all."

"How's that?"

"It, the 'entirety', is the all and the all goes on throughout eternity. Infinite in its capacity. No end, no boundaries yet discovered. But we are talking only of our star, the Sun, and our solar system in relation to life on other planets. So, you believe that there is life out there? Is that life similar to ours?"

"I would suspect so."

"What makes what we are talking about believable?"

"I don't understand. What makes it believable?"

"Nothing. That is what I am getting at. The fact that you believe something does not make it so. There are those, those in the scientific community, those who believe in U F Os and extraterrestrials. But believing in them, even with a PhD in astrophysics, may lend creditability to the belief. It is still only that, a belief, a belief with no basis in fact. What type of life would you believe these ETs to have?"

"Similar to our life. Comparable to Earth. Much like our solar system. A distance from its sun for the planet to sustain life."

"What would they look like?"

"Much like us. Maybe like those people found at Roswell. If, that is, anyone or anything was found at Roswell, New Mexico? I cannot imagine anything much different from the humankind on our Earth today, us. They would look like us, I guess."

"So, you believe they would live in a like environment, a like atmosphere?"

"Yeah. I guess so. But that is only a guess. No more proven than the UFOs. Is that what you are getting at?"

"Indeed. ETs and UFOs have yet to be proven to exist."

"What about all those photos?"

"Many are bright lights against the camera lens. And all the photos of saucers, flying saucers, have been enhanced. It is not important to talk of that which is not provable. But it illustrates one very important point."

"Keep goin', I'm taking notes."

"If no one landed here with human likenesses, how did we get here? If that question can be answered definitively, there would be few follow-up questions. So, it is not a matter of where we began, but how we began."

I'm seeing what you are getting at, I think. Please, go on."

"It is not proof if we cannot prove humans came here from elsewhere, therefore we were created here. The inverse of that would be to say if we can't prove we were created here, we must have come from somewhere else."

"That I understand. But is that not how the ages of the Earth are deciphered? We can tell the age of the crust of the Earth by the sediment and the fossils in it or we can tell the age of the crust of the Earth by the fossils and their depth in the sediment. One proves the other."

"Or disproves the other. But that is geology. A little out of my league. But that does make a good case. Now, let me go on and ask you if you think the cycles of life on another planet would be about the same as ours?"

"By that, I take it you mean lifespan, illnesses, war, pestilence, famine and death."

"Line up those four horsemen. But yes, that is what I meant. So, you believe the planet would be a replica of Earth? And life would be about the same?"

"Yes, but nothing to prove it though."

"That is true. I just need a point of reference for my theory."

"Your theory?"

"Yes, I have a theory that I believe will explain why life did not come to this planet from elsewhere, from another planet."

"What is the difference between a theory and a guess? I guess there might be life on another planet or planets. I could say that because there is life here, it is possible to be elsewhere under like conditions and the trillions of solar systems seems to present a pretty good chance of that being so. My ET theory is based on a guess. You could say Einstein had a guess of relativity."

"Yes, but Einstein was a scientist."

"So, then, a scientist has a theory and a layperson has a guess?"

"'Bout sums it up. A lot of guesses out there in the form of theories. It just gets you published. Theories have creditability. A guess would not. And there is no fine line. A guess is a guess. Why have we not proven that we can bend time? Under Einstein's theory of relativity, we can travel and age less because of the bend in time."

"But don't you have to go faster than the speed of light? And, I understand that nothing is faster than the speed of light."

"Nothing has been measured to be faster than the speed of light. Yet."

"So, until we can travel faster than the speed of light, Einstein's theory will remain just that, a theory?"

"Precisely. Einstein guesses about the bend in time. Oh, we know light bends. We have measured that. And those scientists who had theories of light bending had their theories proven. From a guess to a fact. It takes four years to travel four light years. How would you sustain life for four years in a craft that is on the way at the speed of light?"

"You would have to have a biosphere to replicate the Earth's atmosphere. And only a limited number of people in it at that."

"But we would have to course through space at the speed of light. The space shuttle travels through our bit of outer space at five miles per second. That is almost thirty thousand kilometers per hour."

"My next question is—where are we going?"

"Great question. You are really taking to this. The closest star is

Proxima Centauri. That star, or that sun of the Alpha Centauri solar system, is thirty-nine point nine trillion kilometers from us or two point four light years away."

"A little over two years. Doable."

"At the speed of light. At the speed of our space shuttle, it would take one hundred-fifty thousand years for them to get to us. That is one bad biosphere."

"Oh."

"Indeed. What does that tell you?"

"Let me think a minute."

"Take your time. There is a point I am trying to make for you."

"What this tells me is that it is highly unlikely that a living being traveled to Earth and populated it eons ago."

"Yes."

"Therefore, your theory of the population of the Earth being created is actually stronger than the theory of the ETs and UFOs."

"That is what I wanted you to see. One hundred fifty thousand years of travel is impossible for a living organism, as we know it. And if life on Earth came from other planets, would they not be living organisms as we are?"

"I see your point. What galaxy is Alpha Centauri in?"

"Our galaxy, the Milky Way."

"You mean that the closet solar system to ours is two point four light years away. How big is the galaxy?"

"From our sun to the center of the Milky Way is thirty-five thousand light years. The diameter of the Milky Way is measured to be one hundred thousand light years. It takes our solar system two hundred fifty million years to complete one orbit within the Milky Way at a speed of two hundred fifty-four kilometers per second."

"And there are trillions of galaxies?"

"Yes. I want you to grasp that this discussion is still about the Earth and the creation of life on it. But you have got to have perspective. The immensity of the 'entirety' is hard to comprehend."

"Maybe not for you. But for me, yes."

"Oh, contraire. The more we discover the immenseness of it all, the more the scientific community is awed."

"Think of our limits. It's almost as if we are captured by our inability to venture out any further than we have. We are prisoners of Earth."

"Essentially. But just think of what we have done just in the last hundred years. From the internal combustion engine to the astrophysics of travel into orbit around our planet. From Kitty hawk to the space shuttle."

"How important is it, really? How is it important that we travel to other planets? How important is it that we traveled to the moon?"

"Look at all the discoveries. In the fifties, we had land line telephones that if you wanted to call long distance, you needed an operator. Now, we have cell phones. Think of the medical advances. Lasers. We are always expanding. Searching. The search into new frontiers, the quest for knowledge is a human trait. And we will keep going. What we have discussed today is the ground work for our discussion tomorrow."

"Different topic?"

"Yes, we are going to talk about ages. Time lines. The depth and the magnitude of the process of creation. But for today, I think we have had enough."

"An assignment for tomorrow?"

"Let me think how best to prepare you. You reviewed one day, another day and so on. You may want to review them, again. And go to the second creation, the concept, when it is all in a period much less than the first creation of thought and idea. You will have a lot of questions on the morrow, I am sure. But for now, I think we have used the day wisely, don't you?"

"Yes, I have really enjoyed it. So, tomorrow at nine?"

"Nine it is."

Fiat Lux

"Let there be daytime. Fiat lux in Latin. It is perhaps one of the phrases of the bibles that are not vague in interpretation."

"Bibles?"

"In many versions, it is interpreted 'let there be light'. In its pure form it has a connotation of brightening the earth. Letting light form in that element of 'entirety' that apportions illumination upon our little planet."

"You sound like you are going somewhere with this. Trying to lead me into something. You are good at that, you know. I have a problem with that phrase. It appears to be redundant to the fourth day. Here we have daytime on the opening of the creation, yet on the fourth day, the sun, the moon and the stars are created. Each of the three gives illumination to the Earth. What was created on that first day to let there be daytime?"

"Nothing."

"Nothing?"

"As in no thing. Nothing physical."

"Is not light physical?"

"Yes, there are particles of light. Light is matter. But I am talking of the creation of the soul."

"Keep goin'."

"The soul is the mind, the thoughts, the conscience, the morality of humankind. It is through the soul that we communicate everything to one another. Body language is even via the soul. The soul is the center of being. The soul is the living being on Earth. When your body and brain die, your soul, that which is not matter, moves to another plane.

It is at this instance that your soul passes on to spirit. You lose the soul of your mind."

"Do we not have a spirit now?"

"Spirit and soul are frequently used interchangeably and that is incorrect. On the Earth, your spirit and soul are separate but within one as in body, mind and spirit—Ham, Japheth and Shem. In the mind is the soul, within the matter of the brain; that which gives us thought. The spirit of us is the life force. Physiologically we are alive but the life force that keeps us before we are dead is our spirit. You might think of it as this—the mind, the brain and its functions keep the soul while the body is alive and when the body dies the soul of the mind, less the thoughts of morality and emotion, leaves with the life force, the spirit."

"Yesterday you had mentioned that we are going to talk about ages. I am sure you are getting there, but I am having trouble making the connection."

"We will get there. I want you to understand the soul-spirit connection. Soul and spirit are not interchangeable."

"Can a spirit be without a soul?"

"Yes, I like the way you think. You seem to get out ahead of me and then wham you are all over it. Indeed, a spirit can exist without a soul. The soul is where we begin. The Gehova gave us a soul before we were created in the form of a human. Adam and Eve had a soul but had no spirit until after they died. The first to be created was the soul. The Earth was void and there was nighttime on the surface of the deep."

"What you are getting to is that the emptiness and darkness was a lack of soul. There was no soul on Earth. Am I on the right path?"

"Indeed you are. Allow me to digress. The age of enlightenment is considered to be the seventeen hundreds. It was during these times that a sense of morality overcame the then modern world. Laws, courts, governments and institutions realized the rights of common man to live in a world free of abuse. I know abuse is a tough word, but I have no other way to put it. And of course the enlightenment did not include everyone."

"Slaves."

"Right. But it was a start. In a way, it was a soulful move to greater morality. But it did not relieve that which was immoral."

"The void and the nighttime."

"So, with our understanding of the soul and the relationship thereof, we can proceed to...or...return to the very first of the creation. In the beginning of Iawah's creation of heaven and the Earth, keep in mind that the reference to heaven pertains to the atmosphere and the skies. The matter of air; Iawah is only creating the earth in thought and idea. We, and this is a hard one to swallow, we are only concerned with the creation of the Earth and nothing else. This is the only thing the creation deals with. I have untold stories of how people are put off by this. Some have become insulting and enraged. But with the understanding of this fine point are we able to fully understand the creation. It is our world; the environs of humankind that was created. Only the Earth. The Gehova saw that the Earth was void and of nighttime. I tell you the Earth was here before the beginning of The Gehova's creation. The Earth was in fact formed into a sphere and did at one time contain life, but in the beginning there was nothing. It was void and nighttime."

"Whoa. This is profound. It's as if Iawah had a separate agenda for Earth. That all that was created for us was the Earth. What about the stars and the moon and the sun? How was it not that the sun was made to shine and give the Earth light?"

"It was not that kind of light."

"You mean to tell me I have been getting this wrong all along? The light was enlightenment? That The Gehova gave the Earth enlightenment? It was the first of all the creating? The Gehova gave us a soul? Gave Earth the soul? And all this before the first day was created?"

"So many scientists and theologians get caught up in the day thing. Was one day twenty-four hours or were those first days eons of time? A day is a day and that is why the interpretation. Remember Helel talking about the modern calendar and what a day was. Well, the creation was not written about until there was a written word, about six thousand years ago. And in the original tongue the word Yom was used. Yom means day. But in the original tongue Yom meant time. So, you can make your own determination. But, so simple an answer that a day meant thousands of years is very simplistic. This is why it is very important to get the interpretation correct as to a day, another day, and so on. It is not the second, or third or fourth day, as has been interpreted by many versions. It is a subtle difference as we shall see."

I know you have had me go over that, those days several times, you and Helel. I think I am grasping the connotation."

"As you will, Sal, as you will."

"All through the creation with Helel, we talked of the spirit. It was not until humankind came through the flood that the spirit was in the progeny of Ham, Japheth and Shem. It was not until Shem that humankind was responsible for its own spirit. Yet, here you talk of only the soul as a life force."

"Adam and Eve had a soul but were corrupted."

"The serpent?"

"Correct.

"So, by their actions... Adam and Eve that is... by their actions, they somehow lost their souls, their determination of good and bad."

"Yes, and it was not until the spiritual wash of the flood that humankind was able to be responsible for their own spiritual development. Men and women lost their souls in the garden, they were led astray by the Nephilim, and then had their lives washed away. And it was the confluence of body, mind and spirit that they were rejoined in the spirit individually. Every human on this Earth has a spirit that is now eternal."

"And it all began with The Gehova's creating the soul upon the Earth before anything else was created. Yet, the Earth was already here in a form. Earth was already an orb, a sphere, a planet."

"Yes, the divine presence hovered upon the surface of the waters."

"So, the Earth was all water?"

"The Earth was all melting ice."

"So, six thousand years ago, the Earth was in an ice age?"

"No, the last ice age was approximately ten thousand years ago and that was the beginning of The Gehova's creating."

"So, the beginning of the creation of Earth was only ten thousand years in the past?"

"That is right."

"What about those who have chronologically worked backwards to give us an exact date of creation? Like four thousand four before the common era on October twenty-three? I've heard that one."

"What makes four thousand years before the common era, the start point?"

"I have no idea at this point. It seems the chronology and the creation have met here today. I have to resolve some of my former understanding with this new information. Please, continue."

"It was during the last ice age that The Gehova created that which was to be an Earth with all those creations on given days. That, and I am reluctant to use this word, but it was on those given days that the world evolved as we know it today. It was ten thousand years ago that The Gehova said, let there be daytime, the illumination of the soul. It was a frozen waste land that The Gehova, in divine presence, hovered upon the surface of the waters. As the waters melted the Gehova went on to create the Earth in the form of soil, water and air. But that is another day. We aren't there yet."

"There was no life on the Earth at the beginning?"

"All life had been frozen out, made extinct by the ice."

"Dinosaurs, Neanderthals. That fits with the extinction theories. What caused the ice age?"

"Volcanic ash, brought on by The Gehova."

"So, the Earth was a snowball."

"Funny you should say that. That is what we call the last ice age—The Snowball."

"We are sort of backwards in our discussion today. The ice age came first and then came the beginning of Iawah's and The Gehova's creation."

"I wanted you to understand that, let there be daytime was enlightenment of the soul. If it was not for that, there would have been no purpose for the creation. There was daytime and there was nighttime, that which is magnificent and that which is not magnificent. From the very beginning was the answer to your quote by Marcellus III."

Smoldering Sphere

"Last night I was thinking about the time lines we talked about and there were several. The creation ten thousand years ago? When did the Earth form?

"According to cosmic microwave background radiation, our best system of measurement, the Earth evolved from matter four point five four billion years ago."

"It was nothing but a fireball then, was it not?"

"True. A hydrogen, helium, molten iron sphere slinging through space."

"So, when did it become habitable?"

"A livable biosphere formed about three point five billion years ago."

"And out of that formed all the plant life and animals and early humans. Who created that?"

"The Gehova."

"Whoa. We have another creation story. How many times did The Gehova create the Earth?"

"Of that I have no record."

"Let me get this straight. The Gehova kept creating and destroying the Earth. Why? Was The Gehova trying to get it right?"

"The Gehova was trying to get us to get it right. Do you not remember when The Gehova promised to never destroy the world again? Do you remember the rainbow? That is because we got it right. We finally got it."

"When The Gehova first created the Earth, did The Gehova create the entirety at the same time?"

"No, the Earth is much younger than the 'entirety'. The 'entirety' began thirteen point seven three billion years ago. The Earth is much younger."

"How did that come about? The beginning of the 'entirety' had to start somewhere. Infinite has no beginning. Finite does have a beginning.

"It does not matter who agrees with you. You are correct."

"Can the 'finite', the start, become' infinite'? Can that which began as not eternal become eternal?"

"No, would be my answer to that."

"Then why do we call the 'entirety' infinite?"

"Because it cannot be measured. So the human mind, which has a problem grasping such things a billion of light years, considers the space of the 'entirety' to be 'infinite'."

"How far can we measure? Let me think through this a bit. If we can only measure so far, therefore, the end of our measurement is what we know to be. We know the limits of our measurements and conclude that what is beyond that is' infinite'."

"A bit of faulty reasoning, wouldn't you say?"

"I can't measure it, so it must go on forever. Not too deep, is it? I can find fault with that myself."

"Scientists get rather indignant when you do that. As a matter of fact, scientists hate when you remind them their theories are just that. Theories."

"Couldn't you say that all these microwave measurements are just theories?"

"Not really. Measurements in short distances are accurate. Allowing for some inaccuracy over longer distances. We are in the ball park, so to say. And at these distances, what does a half a billion matter?"

"I see your point. What is the edge of what is measurable?"

"The greatest distance between measurable galaxies is ninety-three billion light years, end-to-end."

"Whoa. Another, whoa. How can something go ninety-three billion light years and are only thirteen point seven three billion years? That would be faster than the speed of light. I thought nothing can go faster than the speed of light."

"Remember, we have never measured anything faster. If something does go faster, we have not picked it up, yet. The 'entirety' expanded with no limit on its rate and no measurement by us beyond the speed of light."

"If we can only measure, or have only measured that far, would the measurement be valid by the expansion of the 'entirety'?"

"As the 'entirety' expands, we may be able to measure further out if we can measure the distance and expansion of those galaxies within the ninety-three billion light years. That is also an explanation as to how the expansion took place within the speed of light. Follow along, now. Take two golf balls and place them on a table about six inches apart. Now, move them away from the center of the table together, but at the same time move them away from each other. The distances expand as the galaxies expand. This is the way the 'entirety' is expanding. The whole is pulling away from the center as the galaxies are expanding one from the other. This is the only clear explanation we have for the time line of the expansion."

"I now have a time-line on the creation. The Gehova created and destroyed the Earth over and over. The last creation was ten thousand years ago and since the Earth is over five billion years old, I can only assume that ice ages and floods came and went. That is what gives us the strata of sediment in our formation of the Earth's crust. This is all becoming clear. The Gehova created it all, just not at once and not in six days. How is it then that we have the six thousand year and not a ten thousand year measurement?"

"That is a good question and a subject for tomorrow. Enough for today."

"Agreed."

The Written Word

"Yesterday we did not talk about the disparity between the theories of the Earth being created about four thousand years before the common era and the reformation of the Earth circa eight thousand years before the common era or ten thousand years ago. Four thousand years is a big swing, a big minus."

"I am going to give you a little lesson on the written word and that will explain the difference. The idea that the Earth was created four thousand years before the common era is incorrect. I must be that succinct. Have you ever heard of proto-writing?"

"Can't say as I have."

"Proto-writing is the use of mnemonic symbols, pictures essentially. Forms of proto-writing go back as far as the seventh millennium before the common era, as early as the Neolithic period. The symbols increased in complexity through the sixth and fifth millennium. Hieroglyphic scripts, including the counting form known as Cuneiform, emerged out of Egypt. Writing emerged in the Bronze Age in different forms. The Bronze Age was in the fourth millennium. So, you see that sophisticated writing began in the fourth millennium and it is from those writings that we have the creation story. Creation did not begin four thousand years before the common era. The recorded history of the creation began four thousand years before the common era, six thousand years ago. Until then, the stories of the creation were written in the crude form of proto-writing. But more than writing, the creation was passed down in the form of storytelling. So, four thousand years before the common era, the stories were captured in writing and eventually into the original tongues. It is from the original tongues that we have the Ricci Version in its form today."

"How would that differ from the original tongues?"

"Modern languages have words written phonetically with modern characters. Also, vowels and tenses have been added. In essence, the interpretation would not be the same. We are interpreting from the oldest written word of the creation. The original tongue is the only language that has survived."

"So, let me get this straight. The written word of creation is what some use to define when the creation began. It is rather simplistic. It makes sense as to the time line going from the ice age ten thousand years ago, to the written word about the events, evolving into modern language."

"The Ricci New Age Version is just that, a version. There are hundreds of versions of the bible, all very far from the correct interpretation of the creation. Many versions were taken from the original tongue, to Greek, to Latin, to German and finally into the English of that time, which you must admit, is far from the way in which we speak it today."

"A lot can be lost in translation by doing that, I am sure. But by taking it from the original tongue to English as the Ricci Version does...well...isn't there a chance of still losing some of the meanings?"

"Yes, there is. What we have in our studies, you, me and Helel is the best we can do."

"Like the days. The original tongue is interpreted a day, another day and another day, etcetera. But some versions interpret the days to be the first day, the second day, but the Ricci Version uses another day. We have come to this subject before, but have not expanded upon it. Why?"

"I wanted you to first understand that the Earth was not created from the beginning of the sphere being formed. The Earth we live upon, the Earth before our time was created over and over until it came to be that upon which we are living. The Earth was created out of matter and The Gehova then gave it life, over and over. These ice ages were all part of the wiping out of all existing life. No one was left. Humankind was not within the spirit of The Gehova that created them. They had free will, but never walked in the Garden of Eden. The way in which they were wiped out was the eruption of volcanoes and the blotting out of the sun. They were not drowned, they were frozen. We still have a record of them today with the discovery of relics and fossils."

"Was humankind as it is today? We have discovered so many different forms. It seems an evolution."

"I am careful in using that word. Humankind did go through periods of being less developed. Each of these evolutions came with the rebirth from an ice age, from the creation by The Gehova."

"It almost sounds as if it is serial creationism."

"It has been. The difference is Noah. In the past creations, the whole world was wiped out as no one of Noah's reputation was to be found. So the volcanoes spewed forth lava and blotted the skies with ash and smoke. The sun could not penetrate and the Earth became a frozen wasteland. Not even the sea creatures survived."

"How many ice ages do we know about?"

"There are plenty of theories out there. But beyond six, we cannot measure. All of the ages, as we say, were not caused by an ice age. All sediment measurements are not from volcanic ash, but most do come from eruptions in the Earth's crust."

"So we have no idea of all the times the Earth was frozen over to wipe out humankind?"

"No. But we do know it was wiped out at least six times."

"Seven creations?"

"Correct."

The Days

"Today we are going to get to the days, a day', another day and another day. This is a continuation of the time line we began yesterday."

"I've been wanting to get to this."

"I think with all that you have learned over the last couple of days and with Helel's notes, you can now distinguish the difference between what you thought to be true and now know to be true. The information you are gathering will be an awaking. And it must be given in small measure to avoid bringing too much heat upon yourself, go slow. Rather than publishing one book, perhaps two would be better, one of Helel and one of our studies. Although we are fortunately beyond the stone-throwing age, what you publish goes against what has been written to date. That is a heavy load, but we picked you because you knew there was something more to be understood about life since you wanted answers to your quote. Being a crime reporter, most will be skeptical, even consider your work blasphemy. Please do not give up in getting to the truth of creation. Keep writing your feature articles but do lectures. Start locally and as the word gets out, do small lecture tours. We want nothing but success for you."

"Thank you."

"You may want to drop the references to the versions of the bible. You do not want to step on too many toes. Beliefs are difficult to overturn. I dare say these studies may be censored in some countries."

"Don't get in too much of a hurry to get this out there."

"Right. The most receptive will be the New Age believers. They are open to daytime being shed on the creation. Start your lectures with New Agers."

"Advice taken. So what about the days?"

"Let's go back to the Earth ten thousand years ago. When the Earth was a huge snowball. The Gehova illuminated the Earth with a soul. There was the brilliance of that which was moral and there was the nighttime, the depths of despair, a day. Some time, ten thousand years ago on a day this came about. The Earth was given a soul from which to develop. Soul, not spirit, was the starting point of the last creation. Soul of morality and emotions and thoughts. Soul was placed on the Earth to guide humankind to that which is magnificent. It took a day to do this."

"Then the oceans and the heavens were created on another day. How far into the time-line this second day was used to create the oceans and the heavens, I do not know. But, it was another day not the second day. It was a day that did not follow a day within a twenty-four hour span. Another day was not the day after a day. Although it could have been. It does not matter except we know only that it was a day and another day of creation."

"Land and vegetation were created on another day. Again, how far along the time-line did this all come about? We only know from the original tongues that is was another day."

"Another day may have followed very closely behind as the life giving rays of the sun were created to shine upon the Earth."

"But was not the sun created prior to the Earth? And were not the other stars created some thirteen billion years ago?"

"You notice that I did not say that the sun, moon and stars were created. They were there. The clouds of the volcanoes were lifted to let them shine through. This was after the heavens were cleared and the rain could wash away the dust and ash. As the Earth's rain clouds formed and the sun was able to warm the Earth. However, the rays of the sun did warm the Earth enough to begin the melting which caused the condensation and thus the clouds and rain. That was the end of another day."

"It is thought that another day followed with some span of time to allow the vegetation to grow enough to sustain life. For on another day, ocean creatures and birds were created."

"Up until now, it is just another day. But into the next day of creation it is called on a sixth day. Why?"

"On a sixth day is a conclusion and may have followed the day before, perhaps two days in a row, perhaps not. This is the day that land creatures and humankind were created, male and female. Keep in mind all of this was done in thought and idea. It was not until the second creation that it was all brought to being as the concept."

"On a seventh day, Iawah rested. A seventh day was when Iawah completed the thoughts and ideas and retired from the creation."

"It was not until an eighth day that The Gehova brought it all together to make the thoughts and ideas come to fruition in terms of our life on this planet one more time."

"An eighth day?"

"It is an eighth day, is it not?"

"That, I need to think about."

"Sal, you have been given a lot of new information to think about in the last couple of days. Mine, along with Helel's, gives you your answers to understand your quote. Not only are we calling it a day…couldn't help but play on the words, this will be our last session."

"*As she extended her hand for a handshake, she wished me well and told me that I had been an excellent student. As I touched her open hand in a gesture to say, thank you, I felt a softness as she, too, disappeared much like Helel had. The room was empty. I was sorry to see the sessions end* as *I walked away from Double A's office to my. I was beginning to feel the enormity of what I had just learned. After a beer in my favorite chair, I sat down at the table, organizing all of my notes, including Helel's, to try to put this all in order. This was a huge puzzle and like a crime reporter that I am, I wanted to put the pieces together to solve the puzzle, to give the answers expected of me.*

I started with the 'entirety' which came to be thirteen plus billion years ago. 'Entirety' was created by The Gehova but not at the same time as the creation of Earth. Earth was eight billion years younger than the 'entirety'. The distances were overwhelming. Our galaxy was one hundred million light years across. The nearest solar system to ours was one hundred-fifty-thousand years away, at the speed of our space shuttle.

Ice ages came and went at the command of The Gehova and it was not until the last ice age ten-thousand years ago the creation, as we know it today, began. Each day is separate from the others in the creation time line and it took eight days for the creation to come from thought to idea to concept.

Soul was the first of The Gehova's creations for the development of humankind. It was soul not spirit that was tested in the garden. Soul being our morality, thought, and emotions—the making of our minds. Our soul on Earth gives us closeness or distance from The Gehova. It was not until the flood and the redemption through Shem did humankind have a spirit and the responsibility for it.

These studies were far from the teachings in many churches. If they believe it or not the readers have to see the whole story. I could think of no other way to tell it. And then I asked myself if this was the last creation. Could there be destruction and creation, again? It was dark and I realized I had been at it long enough. I had a bite to eat and called it a night. I was anxious to get started on my book or books and wanted to start fresh.

And Then There Were Four

I heard the pit-pat of the rain. I opened my eyes and found myself lying on a cot, an army cot. I was covered by a camouflaged blanket. A table was at the end of the tent. A lone lantern was sitting on it. The flickering mantel cast shadows on the tent's walls. The flap at the other end of the tent opened and a man in fatigues came up to the cot. He told me I was wanted in the TOC. From my army days I knew that to be the tactical operations center. I sat up and realized I was dressed in a fatigue shirt, jeans and tennis shoes. This must be a dream, but it felt so real. Around my neck was a name card on a lanyard. I could make out the word press on the card. That was all the man said to me. I got up and walked to the tent flap and took a step outside. The rain hit me in the face and it was then I realized I was not dreaming. I went back into the tent and walked over to the lantern. The card read, 'S Luca—Philadelphia Daily Editor Reporter'. It was signed by someone with the name of 'Israfel'. I felt the heat of the lantern. I was startled but not panicking. The last several days with Helel and Doctor Anael led me to expect anything. I knew this was a continuation of my education. Why and what for, were my questions?

I went back to the tent flap and swung it open. Directly in front of me I could see a large tent, well lit, with several people walking around. I looked around the tent and saw that there was only one cot, mine. I left the tent and walked to the TOC. I entered the TOC and four men in camouflaged fatigues turned toward me. Then three of them turned and walked from the TOC. One approached me and shook my hand.

"Sal, I am General Djibril. Please, come in and have a seat before the map. It's a map of our area of operations.

"It looks to me the map is a map of the world. The world is your area of operations. Djibril! You are the angel Gabriel!"

"Yes, I am Gabriel."

"The big guy." I was really fired up now. Could I be talking to the man? I reached into my pockets and looked for a notebook.

"Don't worry. I know how you work and we will give you a complete transcript of the briefings."

"Briefings?"

"Yes, you are going to be given four briefings. The first one is from me. So, sit back and relax. You may ask any questions you like."

"Whew! I guess I'll start with some questions about you."

"Drive on."

"What is all this? How can you have an operation over the entire world? Are we...I guess I need to ask...who is at war?"

"The whole world is at war."

"Like World War II?"

"Oh, a much greater conflict."

"And you are one of the commanders?"

"One of the four."

"There are only four commanders?"

"That is correct."

"What brings Gabriel here? And you introduced yourself as Djibril? That is Arabic, is it not?"

"I am one of the highest-ranking angels of Islamic lore. My name means Iawah is my strength. I am the spirit of truth. I inspired Mohammed and Jean D'Arc. I am the angel of mercy and destruction."

"Mercy and destruction. How can that be?"

"We are all a contradiction, the four of us. Is not war a contradiction?"

"When you think of it, yes. It is the ultimate contradiction."

"We are each one of us an alpha and an omega. I am thought of as the angel of revelation. I am also an angel of destruction. I destroyed Sodom and Gommorah."

"You are an archangel, are you not?"

"Yes, one of the four. You shall meet the others tonight, as well."

"Why am I being briefed? And for that matter, where are we and what day is it?"

"We are in the future. But, of course, we are always in the now, are we not? As for the location, we are in the desert. The location would not make sense to you as from your time the countries of the world have changed."

"Changed? How?"

"Collections of countries have become mega nations. You would not recognize the East or Europe. The map of Earth is changed to reflect the brink of conflagration. Each poised to conquer the other. It was only a matter of time before the conflict was started."

"Back to the question. Why am I here?"

"You are the most educated student of the Genesis Encryption."

"Genesis Encryption?"

"It began with your inquiry about the Marcellus III quote. You learned of the thoughts, ideas and concepts. And when it was all finished you moved on to Doctor Anael. Then you asked another question."

"And that was?"

"You asked if the Earth would ever be destroyed. If The Gehova would ever destroy the Earth, again. But, of course, you remember the rainbow. A sign that The Gehova would not cause the Earth to be destroyed—no fires, no meteor showers, no floods, no ice ages."

"So you are saying if the Earth is to be destroyed, it will be at humankind's hand. The destruction, that is. Now, that begs the question. If humankind destroys the world, will The Gehova create it, again?"

"We, the four of us, do not know. Humankind could destroy the

Earth and The Gehova could begin another creation. That is left to humankind and The Gehova, is it not?"

"So it is."

"Let me brief you as to the situation I command."

"Are you involved in a conflict at present?"

"Yes, we are."

"The four of you? What...where is the conflict?"

"The four of us have a different conflict. The conflicts are world wide as you shall see."

"Please, continue...sorry to interrupt."

"Let me get my pointer. Oceania, which consists of Indonesia, Australia, New Zealand and New Guinea became the Oceania Republic. Internal strife began almost immediately. Wage and standard of living disparities are the reason. The poor rose up and martial law was put into effect. The fight continues today as government buildings and homes of the wealthy are razed. The civil war has caused the four islands to collapse and all are now failed states."

"Australia and New Zealand?"

"Why were you shocked at those two?"

"I think of them as more stable."

"The general population lost more wealth in Australia than any other island. Of course they had more to lose. They are in the worst state of collapse. Just about all the modern government services are out of commission. But, let's move on. The United States of Europe, too, are in collapse. When the economically challenged nations of Eastern Europe were brought into the fold, it was not long before the less wealthy, and I use less wealthy, rose up and wanted government services on par with the Western States. All but England and Germany are now failed states."

"How long has this gone on?"

"Nearly a decade. The New Russian Republics are in total economic collapse. Bitter fighting is between all the Republics, one against the other."

"New Russian Republics. Are you telling me the Soviet Union was re-formed?"

"Yes. Now to North America. Mexico, Canada and the United States have formed a Republic. So far the United States and Canada are fairly stable but Mexico is trillions in debt to China and South Korea. Civil strife is occurring more often in the cities. As for the United States, Chicago and Philadelphia have completely broken down. Charlotte, North Carolina has been burned to the ground."

"What!"

"Follow along. The Asian Alliance is where the most stability exists but that is because they have become police states."

"What is your role in all of this?"

"It was for me to cause it."

"What! I'm sorry I keep saying what, but I can't conceive of all this. You are saying that there are only four spheres of influence?"

"That is correct. All the alliances came about at the same time."

"So, you are the commanding general of civil strife?

"Yes."

"That begs the question. Why?"

"I heard one of the voices scream out in a voice of thunder. I heard the voice command, "Civil war"; I looked and saw a white horse. The rider was armed with a bow and had a crown. The rider rode out for conquest and to conquer from within."

"You...the four of you are the four horsemen of the apocalypse?"

"Yes."

"There has to be some connection between the civil wars and you. I take it the white horse has a deeper meaning?"

"I am riding out to conquer from within."

"Why? What brought this on?"

"You did."

"I take it you mean we did?"

"Absolutely."

"Why did the nations divide up in such a fashion?"

"Self interest, spheres of influence...protection."

"Protection from what."

"Selfishness."

"How is that?"

"I can give you an example of the United States. Over seventy percent of the population lives below the poverty level. Over ninety percent of the wealth of the nation is in the hands of less than one percent of the people. And the distribution of wealth in the United States was better than any other country in the world."

"Good grief."

"Yes, good grief. It started with the distribution of wealth and soon declined in a fight for basic needs. Food, of course, is the main reason for the civil strife. Food wars were rampant in all the mega nations. The Asian Alliance armed forces just killed the starving or left them to starve."

"What you are saying is the civil wars could have been avoided, but for greed and food distribution."

"Correct."

"And knowing this, why did you, the four of you, not stop this before it got out of hand? If you could destroy Sodom surely you could have saved these nations from civil war."

"No, we could not. It is up to humankind to save itself from civil wars. The wheat belt of the United States and the rice of China could feed the world, but the food was hoarded and sometimes destroyed to run up the price. Everyone had to face inflation, costs go higher and higher so the controllers of the goods could profit more and more."

"I see. This is what we will do in the future? Can you give me a time? What year is it?"

"The year is to be determined by humankind, not us."

"So, humankind created this situation...you merely command over it. What you are saying is that we have a choice. But now, as of this briefing, we have failed."

"Precisely. If there are no further questions, I will be followed by the red horse."

"Can it be changed?"

"In time, it will be revealed."

And with that, Gabriel lay down the pointer, nodded and walked from the tent. I was left alone. I used the time to gather my thoughts. The world around me was crumbling and this was only a fourth of it. I could not remember the second horse. I knew that the oft quoted, "war, pestilence, famine and death" was not correct. Civil war seemed to be the first horse, the white horse. I was a lone correspondent in a war zone. Normally, I would have a T V hook-up for one of the cable channels. This, too, was surreal. Soon, I was being approached by another man in fatigues.

"Hello, Sal. I am Mikhail, Michael to you."

"Are you a General?"

"Yes."

"And your name means?"

"Who is as Iawah?"

I could see Michael was going to be a short answer interview. "Are you not the lead angel of all angels?"

"I am chief in the order of virtues."

"Which horseman are you?"

"Then another horse appeared. It was red and fiery. Its rider was the taker of peace from the Earth. The rider made men slay one another and had a large sword."

"Fiery red horse. Is there some meaning to the color?

"Yes, I represent communism."

"And what of the communists. I imagine you mean the New Russian Republics that Gabriel talked about?"

"Yes."

"The rider is the taker of peace. Is the New Russia at war?"

"Yes."

"And with whom?"

"The states of the un-unified Middle East."

"I was going to ask about that. It seems that the whole world is divided into four spheres of influence, yet Gabriel said nothing of the Middle East."

"The Middle East is torn apart by strife."

"Sunni and Shiite?"

"Sunni and Shiite, those with oil and those without oil."

"What of Israel?"

"There are fifteen United States divisions in Israel."

"That appears to be about all of the U S A divisions."

"About a fifth."

"The USA built up its military that much."

"The USA had to repel an invasion by The Asian Alliance. It took sixteen divisions to push the Asians back into the sea on the west coast."

"We are at war with China?"

"As a member of The Asian Alliance, yes."

"How is it you are a taker of peace?"

"I command the communist forces that are now marching on the Middle East."

"But why?"

"Oil."

"Does not Russia have plenty of oil?"

"Its supply has dwindled."

"What, the wells dried up?"

"No, the sales to Europe."

"Why so much to Europe?"

"Russia needed the money to fight the civil wars erupting throughout the countries of the republic."

"Russia is now fighting a war in the Middle East and in its states. A civil war and a foreign war?"

"And has for over three years."

"Can you give me an overview of the status of these unions?"

"Of course. Oceania is in a defensive posture hoping to stave off an attack by The Asian Alliance. At one time, an area of New Guinea was occupied but the Australians cut off the supply routes and the Asians were allowed to disengage. Since then, Oceania has been in a military build-up."

"Excuse me, but it seems the whole world is in military build-up."

"That is why I ride the fiery red horse, to bring wars to the world. Soon the whole Earth will explode in a giant conflagration."

"Who started all of this?"

"If I had to point my finger toward the igniter of the state we are in today, I would say Europe and the USA."

"How can that be?"

"By not feeding the needy. Being avaricious and hoarding food from sales. As Gabriel told you this was to make the price go up. But the poor in all corners of the Earth could not pay anything for the food."

"What about Africa? Neither you nor Gabriel said anything about that region."

"Wiped out."

"Wiped out!"

"Yes."

"How can that be? The whole region?"

"AIDS and starvation. Less than one tenth of the population still survives."

"Good grief."

"Indeed."

"How can you do this? Take the peace?"

"Think of it this way. All nations waged defense."

"Waged defense. That is an unusual term."

"Every country on the face of the Earth raised an army for defense and internal control. Even the neutral nations. Every nation was always preparing for a conflict. Always training for the fight. It has now come about."

"Come about?"

"Yes, the fight."

"You are commanding this to occur? The result of preparation for war? But a country has to defend itself. How else could it stay viable? All nations have to defend against aggression."

"My question is why aggress?"

"Because the aggressor wanted something. Is that correct?"

"Precisely."

"In this case oil and food."

"Think about it. It was always about oil and food. Modern armies I mean."

"I see your point. Food first and industry second."

"When you are hungry do you not get edgy?"

"A little testy I guess. I see where you are going. Just think of the hunger of an entire nation."

"It manifests itself into aggression. Starvation is a great motivator."

"Why then did Africa not go to war?"

"Africa had nothing to go to war with."

"I see your point."

"With Africa losing its population the world has decreased in numbers. The Earth's population has gone from six billion to around five point five billion."

"Five hundred million people dead. In how long a span of time?"

"A little over three years."

"Lord!"

"Indeed."

"So civil wars and international conflicts worldwide have been going on for over three years?"

"All nations have been affected. Though India and Latin America less than the great alliances."

"What has left India and South American countries out of this?"

"Self implosion. India has fallen apart internally. The country relied on the USA and Europe too much, and therefore went into economic chaos as the markets dried up. India is starving too, as is Africa. The death toll has been great."

"And Latin America?

"They are having to deal with internal conflicts. Not civil wars. The dictators, and all the countries are now run by dictators, are using their armies to control the population. More will die of murder than will succumb to starvation. No citizen is allowed to leave the borders. The only country not in the throes of despotism is Brazil. Brazil has depth in goods and can hang on. But they too will feel the lack of food, supplies and services within less than a year. The president has declared martial law to protect the citizens."

"I have had so much thrown at me. I have not had time to discuss the four horsemen and where you come from. It is Revelations, is it not?"

"Yes and no."

"Can we start with the no of your answer?"

"It is written in Zechariah in the sixth chapter beginning verse one—**I turned and looked and beheld four chariots coming between mountains. The first chariot was pulled by red horses and the second chariot was pulled by black horses. And the third chariot by white horses, with the fourth chariot pulled by grizzled horses. I heard the call, "What are these, lord?" And the answer was, "These are the four spirits of the other side. The black horses go north and the white horses after them. The grizzled go to the south."**"

"And now can we get to the yes of your answer? Does it take us to Revelations?"

"Yes, it is not of the New Testament as you call it. It is the fulfillment of the four chariots."

"So, north and south has something to do with it? The directions?"

"As you get to the other horsemen, more will be revealed."

"And what of the red horses? Where do they go?"

"It is not written, but the red horses go throughout the world. World war."

"And the four spirits of the other side? Is there a link to the spirits of the other side and the spirit given humankind after the flood?"

"The four spirits mean the four corners of the Earth. The first nether world, in Islamic lore, is the place of the stars and the place of Adam and Eve. The second nether world, in Islamic lore, is the place of Jesus and John the Baptist. This is the nether world where Moses first encountered the angel Nuriel, who was fashioned from water and fire. The third nether world is where the divine bees of manna were brought by me. Both Paradise and Torture are accommodated in this world. Azrael, the angel of death is in the other side. Torture is located on the north side."

"Is this also according to Islamic lore? Jesus in Islamic lore?"

"Yes, read the Koran. Jesus is mentioned scores of times."

"Are you serious?"

"And in the fourth nether world is where Mohammed encountered Enoch."

"Why are you and the others telling me all of this? I thought angels brought good tidings, not all of this."

"You were chosen because you were known for your honest reporting and willingness to continue to work until you find the truth. We are very pleased with our choice."

"I suppose I should say, thank you, but now that I know, I don't know what to say."

"You are welcome will do." With that Michael shook my hand and faded before me.

It was several minutes until the third angel appeared. Azrael was dressed in black fatigues. He came up to me, shook my hand and put his left hand on my shoulder. He motioned for me to have a seat, then picked up the pointer and moved directly to the map.

"Michael, Gabriel and Israfel failed to provide handfuls of Earth for the creation of Adam. I did. So doing, I was awarded a separate body from my soul. I have as many eyes and tongues as there are humans on Earth…I am forever writing the births of man and erasing them at death. I am the angel of the death of billions. In Islam I am another form of Raphael….**and there before me was a black horse. The rider was holding a pair of scales, then heard a loud voice among the four living horsemen, "A quart of wheat and three quarts of barley for a day's wages, and do not waste the wine nor waste the oil!"** I am the third horseman, Azrael.

"A quart of wheat and three quarts of barley for a day's wages. Starvation?"

"Famine. Earthly Famine."

"What I can't understand are the angels that are commanding the armies of destruction. Are angels not the spirits of love and mercy? What hath Iawah wrought?"

"Again, it is not what Iawah wrought, but what humankind hath wrought. Nothing accompanies war or follows war as much as famine. Famine killed millions of Russians, scores of millions of Chinese, North Koreans, Africans, et al. I am the black horseman, I am capitalism."

"I don't understand. Continue, please."

"Who better to end famine than the wealthy? But with the world at war and almost every country waging civil war, who is there to farm? Between Canada and the United States, the world can be fed two times over."

"You, Michael and Gabriel are blaming the capitalists and the communists for all of this?"

"No, there is no blame, only truth."

"So, tell me. How many will die as a result of the famine?"

"Over a billion before the conflagration."

"Conflagration?"

"The great death. We are all death. The four of us."

"That is what I mean. Angels are a saving grace, are they not?"

"How soon you forget. Think of the Nephilim."

"I see your point."

"Angels are all things to all of humankind. Remember the lineage of Ham, Jatheth and Shem? All the conditions of the body, mind, and spirit? Remember?"

"How could I forget?"

"There is angel for each one of those conditions and more."

"How many angels sit on the head of a pin?"

"Cliché, but a good question. The answer is all of us or none of us. Keep in mind, we are always in the now. The time line on the civil wars, the world war and the famine are humankind's. Therefore, the destruction can be stopped at any minute. We, angels are the same as the Nephilim. We are here to serve as guides."

"Some guides. I don't mean to crack wise, but what kind of guidance is this?"

"We are guiding you. You decide what direction you want us to guide. If it is to live in peace, we will guide you in that direction. If it is to feed the world, we are your guidance. With all the conditions of body, mind and spirit you have decided on only four avenues. You are walking down the streets of civil war, world war, famine and death."

As Azrael said that another angel entered the tent. Azrael put down the pointer and saluted me. As he left the tent, the fourth horseman came to the map.

"I am Israfel. I am the burning one. I will blow the trumpet on the day of judgment. I initiated the writings of Mohammad before Gabriel. I am the angel of the end of this Earth."

"At the end?"

"Yes."

"Is there another Earth to follow?"

"That is the choice of Iawah."

"I notice you referred to Iawah, not The Gehova. Are you referring to thought and idea?"

"Very good, Sal."

"What you are saying is that the Earth will be destroyed and made anew. You are saying that the Earth's destruction is up to humankind and the re-creation is Iawah's. Is this as far as we get? We come to this?"

"Not bad, really."

"Not bad!"

"In the scheme of things you, humankind, has lasted a lot longer than the four of us thought."

"How long is long?"

"How long have nuclear weapons been in the arsenals of countries? And yet, for decades and decades they were not loosed. Except, of course, the first three. One in New Mexico and two in Japan."

"I think I know where this is going."

"The fourth living horseman rode a pale horse. Its rider was named death and the other side was following close behind him. He was given power over a fourth of the Earth to kill by sword, famine, plague and the wild beasts of the Earth."

"A pale horse?"

"The Middle East."

"You are going to kill one fourth of the Middle East?"

"No. A fourth of the inhabitants of Earth."

"And you are killing by wild beasts?"

"Tanks."

"I see. But I thought the whole of Earth was to be destroyed. A day of judgment. And where does that come in, the judgment?"

"In this case judgment means certified as in a decree or a legal finding. Not to judge. Iawah or The Gehova never judge."

"I knew that. I guess I am getting a little tired."

"No doubt."

"I'm sorry. But, please, continue.

"In answer to your question about the Earth being destroyed. This time around, during the first nuclear exchange, one quarter of the population that has not starved will be killed. That is when we, the four of us, will leave. The second exchange will burn up all the oxygen in the atmosphere. Earth will be destroyed by fire. It will be the will of Iawah if the Earth is to be created once again as has been done before. Each time humankind advances a little further."

"Further? I don't understand."

"Yes, consider the first humans. They were barely able to provide for themselves with a life expectancy of twenty years. With each creation, The Gehova saw humankind develop consciousness, a spirit and an understanding of its responsibility for its spirit. One thing that will have to be vanquished in the next creation, if there is one, is the idea that war is moral. In a quest for survival, each country improved its defense forces. I should call it the offense forces. Weapons of war were the greatest industry on Earth. That industry destroyed Earth. And there endth your lesson. Write well, Sal. Yours is an awesome burden. You will bear the weight well. I have confidence in that. Good-bye my friend."

It was raining when I woke up. I moved around, getting ready to tackle Helel and Doctor Anael's papers, I couldn't stop thinking about my dream, about the four angels. It seemed so real. When I sat down at my desk, there was an unfamiliar transcript titled, "The Four Horseman." On top of it was a name card that read, 'S Luca—Philadelphia Daily Editor Reporter', signed by Israfel attached to the lanyard which I remembered wearing during the briefings. I skimmed through the pages of the transcript. It appeared each of the interviews were there, as promised. I would not change a word of it.

The Calvary

With so much information, I needed a break. I headed to my favorite place that served breakfast twenty four hours a day. The four horsemen were still fresh in my mind. I had met the ultimate cavalry. The four most dangerous angels of the creation. Gabriel, Michael, Azrael and Israfel. Four angels of Arabic lore. As I thought about it, as I had been briefed, all roads led to the Middle East. The thing was, I had no time line on all of this. But no matter. The time was not as important as the result. I could take it as the end or I could take it as a warning. When I got back to my apartment, I saw an unfamiliar disc on the table. It's label read, "Interviews with Helel, Anael, Gabriel, Michael, Azrael and Israfel. I put it in my computer and there was Helel on my laptop screen. Here was everything I needed to write the story of how I had been given the answers to understand the quote, "If we have not discovered that which is not in us, that which is in us cannot be found." I was anxious to get started. I thought about putting the cavalry first because I felt it was important for me to give the warning. But with second thought, I realized I had to publish in the order that I had been given the lessons. I was going to do the three books, in sequence, in the order of my meetings with each of the angels. I knew some would consider it heresy. But I also knew that it being the truth, many would believe. My ultimate hope was that it would be understood before it was too late.

Postscript

I had a great time writing Genesis Encryption. This is a novel. The book Earth Alone and The Ricci New Age Version of the bible are fictional. Also, there is no netopedya.com. The version of scripture used in Genesis Encryption is mine. There are no direct quotes from any literary works. I did garner considerable information from the on-line encyclopedia, wikipedia.org, and I want to give that publication credit. There is no Marcellus III.